Nicole Varnam started writing when she was twenty-two years old. It started with her main character Noah and progressed from there. The small town in the Yorkshire Dales where she grew up provided inspiration for the setting. She was working full-time when she started writing, but always found the time to for it.

She hopes readers will enjoy this book as much as she enjoyed writing it.

NOAH MOON

THE RETURN OF THE VAMPIRES

Nicole Varnam

NOAH MOON
THE RETURN OF THE VAMPIRES

Olympia Publishers
London

www.olympiapublishers.com
OLYMPIA PAPERBACK EDITION

A CIP catalogue record for this title is
available from the British Library.

ISBN: 978-1-84897-337-4

(Olympia Publishers is part of Ashwell Publishing Ltd)

This is a work of fiction.
Names, characters, places and incidents originate from the writer's imagination.
Any resemblance to actual persons, living or dead, is purely coincidental.

First Published in 2013

Olympia Publishers
60 Cannon Street
London
EC4N 6NP

Printed in Great Britain

I would like to dedicate this book to my family,
who have supported me and always been there for me.

One

Noah Moon woke suddenly. Another bad dream, it was the fifth one this week. The nightmares had begun a couple of weeks ago, he'd never had them before really. As the week had gone on they had got more frequent and a lot worse. The nightmares were strange to him, at first he thought they meant something, but this one was the most confusing. He wasn't sure exactly but he was convinced he'd dreamt about vampires and werewolves. He sat up to think, tried to get the images back into his mind, but it didn't work. He turned over to look at his bedside clock, 4.00 a.m., just three more hours and he had to be up for school. He got up to get a glass of water, as he walked across his room a beam of light illuminated his room. He looked out of the window assuming it was a car, but it had gone. He thought maybe it was his father coming home from the night shift. His father Greg was a police officer and he'd always preferred working at night. Noah gulped the glass of water in one, and went back to bed, and tried to fall back to sleep.

It felt as though he'd just got to sleep when his alarm rang; he grunted and pressed the snooze button. He wanted just five more minutes; he pulled the covers over his head.

"Noah time to get up!" His mother, Anne, always had to shout him up. Unlike his mum and older sister Roxy, Noah wasn't a morning person. He grunted for a second time followed by a yawn as he rolled out of bed. He walked or more staggered into the bathroom and looked at his reflection in the mirror. He noticed dark half circles appearing under his light blue eyes. He also looked pale, the light brown tan he normally had seemed to be fading more and more every morning. He looked as though he was run down with the flu, but apart from the overwhelming tiredness he felt fine. The nightmares were making it so he hardly got any sleep. Not only was it affecting how he looked, his school work was also suffering. And if his dad knew he would be furious. Greg was a father who preferred his children to get straight A's. Roxy wasn't really bothered about her school work. She wanted to leave school at 16, but her father made her stay in sixth form for two years. She was glad that she was now in her last year. That as it was, Greg put all his pressure on Noah. He saw a pile in the corner of his room, he fished out what he needed and threw them on. He left his room and closed the door behind him. He made his way downstairs and into the kitchen. His family had already started eating. He was surprised to see his dad at the table as he normally went straight to bed.

"Morning Dad, you just got in?" Noah asked as he sat down to a plate of sausages and bacon, Noah didn't have an egg like the others, he wasn't keen on them he never had been.

"Yeah it was a busy night," Greg answered while taking sips of his coffee. Anne got up to start clearing the dishes; she was a typical mother and housewife and she was the last one to get her food but the first to finish and start cleaning the kitchen before the others had finished. But just lately Noah was the last to the breakfast table. She put her plate and the pans she'd used into the sink and turned on the tap; she put her fingers under the running water to check if it was getting warm enough to squirt some washing up liquid into it. She glanced over her shoulder at Noah, she noticed he was picking at his food, and didn't seem interested in eating it, which wasn't like him.

"Noah, are you feeling OK?" she asked.

He looked up from his plate to answer. "Yeah fine, just didn't get much sleep last night."

"Well you look like death," she replied. Noah hadn't told his parents about his nightmares; he didn't want to worry them, especially his mother, she was the worrying kind. And she always read too much into the little things. And both his mum and dad seemed to have enough on their minds just lately.

"You ready to go?" Roxy said as she stood up and pushed her chair back under the table.

"Yep," Noah replied while grabbing a sausage off his plate. Roxy always drove him to school. It was just about the only time they spent together, so in a way he enjoyed it. He followed his sister out the door, picking up his rucksack off the floor.

"Bye you two, have a great day," their mother called behind them. Noah went round to the passenger side opened the door and threw his rucksack on the back seat and climbed in. Roxy was already sat in the driving seat and had the engine running. As soon as he shut the door she eased out of the driveway and turned right. She glanced at Noah as she did; he was half asleep with his head resting against the window.

"Did you have another nightmare?"

"Yeah no big deal, they will pass soon." He realised at that point his eyes were fully closed. Roxy was the only person he spoke to about his nightmares, well apart from his best friend Lucy, he told her everything.

"You should tell Mum you know."

"Why?"

"And you should definitely tell Dad, maybe he can help."

"How will Dad be able to help?" He opened his eyes slightly, and then they closed again.

"He probably went through the same thing before he turned…" She cut off her sentence realising she'd already said too much. Noah got a slight boost of energy and sat up straight in his seat.

"Before he turned what, what'd you mean?" Roxy was panicking she didn't know what to say. She eventually said the first thing that came into her head.

"Seventeen, before he turned 17, it maybe genetic."

"Nightmares, genetic, I don't think so!" He loved the fact that he was much more intelligent than she was, and it didn't take much on her part for him to mock her. Roxy was more interested in the gossip going around school and also keeping a reputation of being a bitch, because of this she barely spoke to him at school. She just associated herself with a specific group of people, which on occasion Noah found odd. Especially since some of the boys his sister was friends with bullied him in a way. They didn't do it every day or even every week, they just seemed to go through phases of targeting him.

"Just making a suggestion, wouldn't want the swot's school work to get affected!" she snapped back. She paused for a moment and glanced at him, she could tell that hadn't got to him so she carried on. "They're just dreams anyway, what's so scary about a dream, that you don't even want to fall asleep." That's what got to him, when Roxy started she pushed and pushed until he got really mad.

"They just are alright; I don't want to talk about it any more."

"Yeah not to me but I'll bet you'll tell your girlfriend all about it!"

Roxy had noticed Lucy walking towards school as she'd turned the corner to park the car.

"She's not my girlfriend, some people can just be friends with the opposite sex unlike your group; whose turn is it this month, Alex or Tyler?" Roxy was beginning to become enraged. Noah got out the car before she could start again. He walked with a quick pace towards Lucy who was waiting by the tree. As he did he thought about what Roxy had said about him and Lucy, she wasn't entirely off key. Lucy wasn't his girlfriend, but he wanted her to be. He had loved her since he was 14 years old, but had been best friends with her since they started school. He felt that because of their friendship he couldn't tell her, either that or he was too afraid to. As he walked he thought in the back of mind that there was something Roxy wasn't telling him about their father, and he certainly wasn't buying her tale on turning 17. He shrugged the thought as he reached Lucy. She had her back to him; he tapped her on the shoulder when he was close enough. She turned around and smiled; when she did Noah felt his heart skip a beat. At night when a nightmare woke him he thought about her smile to help him sleep. As he smiled back he tried to absorb all her beauty, like taking a photograph in his mind. Her silky brunette hair, that reached just below her shoulders, her pouty plump lips, which had a glossy pink coating from her lip-gloss. He stared into her dark brown eyes, so dark they looked mysterious, and he felt he got lost in them. Lucy's mother was Spanish-Filipino, so she had inherited her golden brown skin. Her name was actually Lucille, but she preferred Lucy.

"Hey Noah, you OK!" As she spoke her smile faded into look of worry. "You have another nightmare?" It took him some time to reply.

"Oh yeah I'm fine though, how about you?"

"Yeah my mum and dad were fighting again last night, and this morning," she replied as they started walking towards school.

Lucy was an only child, and lately she was worrying about her parents fighting, which was a lot. Because she was worrying about her parents Noah didn't want her worrying about him and his stupid nightmares; he kept telling her that they would soon pass, even though they were getting worse. The silence had gone on too long. Lucy decided to break the tension. "Shall we meet Jack now or in class?"

"We'll see him in class," Noah replied after a moment, he wanted to spend as much time alone with Lucy as possible. And as Jack was the only person who knew about his true feelings for Lucy, he knew he'd understand.

They finally made it to class. Jack was sat in his usual place, just as they turned into the door he was sat against the wall. The three started exchanging answers to homework and comparing essays. When the bell rang for their first class, they shoved their books back into their bags and made their way down the corridor to the English department. Mr Fisher their English teacher was sat at his desk; he glanced from his paperwork to see the students enter. Noah looked at him; he could tell he was losing interest more and more in the way he looked. The smartly dressed clean-shaven man was now looking scruffy, he hadn't shaven in a while and his clothes were tatty. He'd also stopped wearing contacts and his half circled glasses were on the end of his nose and made him look older than he was. Noah and his friends sat three rows from the front. Noah sat nearest the wall and rested his head against it. As Mr Fisher rose up from his seat to address the class, Noah felt himself drifting off to sleep. The noises in room and around him slowly drifted away. And a tall man came into

16

focus. His hair long and dark, reaching almost to his hips, his eyes seemed red, and his skin was very pale, as though this man had never seen sunlight. Someone out of picture said his name, but Noah couldn't hear him clearly enough to tell what it was. The man in front of him began to speak. Only certain words were said clearly, enough to know that he was talking about something he was looking for. Noah heard his name in the distance.

"Noah, Noah!" He opened his eyes to see Mr Fisher standing in front of his desk. "I have had enough of you falling asleep during my lessons, fall asleep in my time, you can do the work in your time, in detention!"

"Sorry sir," Noah replied.

"I should think so, I trust you have your homework!" Noah immediately rummaged in his bag, when he found what he was looking for he pulled it out and handed it to Mr Fisher.

"You two, your homework!" Mr Fisher addressed Lucy and Jack.

"I don't have it!" said Jack.

"Me neither," Lucy answered.

"Well, well, my three best students all in detention, together," said Mr Fisher He went to go sit at his desk. He placed the work he'd collected from the rest of the class in his briefcase, and continued his lesson.

The day went slowly; when the bell rang for lunch Noah thought at first that it was home time. He looked up at the clock and sighed. He strolled down the corridor to the canteen, and joined the long queue. Lucy and Jack had already got theirs and were sat waiting for Noah. He searched the hall to locate where they were sat; as he did he also spotted Roxy at her usual table with her usual crowd. When he finally got his lunch, he'd planned a route through the tables to avoid them. But it didn't work. Joel quickly saw him and headed in his direction.

"Hey wimp, I heard that you get scared at dreams!" Joel bellowed in his face. Noah looked straight at Roxy and gave her the dead eyes. Joel was a tall stocky guy; it was obvious he lifted weights. He always wore tight T-shirts that made it seem as though his biceps were going to rip through the fabric. He had dark hair that reached down to cheeks, his four friends were the same except with different coloured hair. Even though they were good friends with his sister, they had bullied him for years. And she never stuck up for him, and that hurt Noah. He'd got used to it now so he just ignored their comments. They just eased through school as if it wasn't important; they never listened during lessons, and were constantly getting detention. Just like Noah they also fell asleep in lessons, they never did their homework. Nobody dare tell them what to do, the teachers seemed nervous about telling them when they did have detention. Most of the time they got out of it, it was by far strange. Noah pushed past Joel and joined Lucy and Jack at their table.

"Going to go cry over dreams are you!" said James, he then laughed and high-fived Joel and the others, including Roxy. Noah glanced over but didn't stare, he didn't want to give them the satisfaction of realising they'd got his attention and were bothering him. He ate his lunch without speaking, he didn't know what to say, so they both kept quiet too. Eventually home time came, Lucy waited with Noah by Roxy's car, she always took her time. He never understood it; she never wanted to go in mornings, and yet when it was time to go home she was always the last to leave the building.

"Here she comes I'll see ya on Sunday," Lucy said as she noticed Roxy walk out the main entrance with her band of friends not too far behind. They said their goodbyes as they parted ways, and Roxy kept her eyes on Lucy as she strutted towards her car. Lucy noticed her stare and gave her the dead eyes back. They didn't like each other, they never had. Then again only a few people other than her friends actually liked Roxy, others were afraid of her as she had a reputation for being rather nasty to anyone outside of her little click, including him. Roxy got in the car and started the engine. Noah realised if he didn't get in quick she'd drive off and leave him to walk home, and it was a fair way back home on foot, as he had found out once. Roxy had been mad at him for telling one of the teachers about a prank her and her friends had planned; she'd called him a traitor amongst other things. She'd driven off before he could get in the car, and it had started raining. Noah had walked miles, before Roxy had confessed to their parents where he was, and their father picked him up. But by the time Greg had found him he was soaked and all Roxy could do was laugh.

He quickly opened the door and jumped in, throwing his bag on the back seat. Roxy's bag was now on the floor. He had to shove it off the seat and onto the floor in order to sit down; when he'd climbed in he kicked it from under his feet.

"Do you mind?" she snapped as she reversed out of the parking space and drove out of the car park. He ignored her and looked out of the window. They set off down the High Street in silence. She kept glancing at him, eventually she broke the silence.

"I'm sorry about what happened at lunch with Joel."

"No you're not, why did you tell them about it?" he replied in the angriest voice he could manage.

"I didn't, they just knew."

"Sure they did!" Noah said sarcastically.

19

"There will come a day when they won't treat you like that."

"Oh really and how do you know!" He was getting angrier the more she spoke, he just wanted her to shut up and leave him alone. She didn't realise it wasn't Joel and the others that bothered him, it was her.

"No reason I just know." She was doing it again playing mind games, trying to make him probe into what she meant or was hiding, just like that morning, but he wasn't going to bite this time. They continued their journey in silence.

Two

When Noah stepped into the house, leaving Roxy in the car to talk on her mobile, he heard his parents talking in the kitchen. He was just about to open the door and greet his parents, but instead found himself pressing his ear against it to listen in.

"I don't think so Greg, not yet, you only have to wait until Sunday!" his mother said, she sounded worried and anxious.

"I understand your concern, I do, but the others insist he needs to know now!" Greg replied.

"No, he's my son and it'll just have to wait."

Noah gasped as he realised they were talking about him. He thought at first they were talking about his birthday, which was on Sunday. But it didn't make sense. Why did his mother sound worried and anxious if that was the case? And he was curious to find out what had to wait. They were quiet for a moment until Anne continued.

"What difference will it make anyway?"

"It will just make it easier for him, that's all," Greg replied. "You don't know how difficult it is at first, you don't know what's happening until you finally decide to tell someone, and with that there's the risk he may tell his friends and we can't take that risk, you know that."

"You don't think I know that, Roxy has told me he tells those two everything, but there has to be a better way!"

"Speaking of Roxy when it was her time you couldn't wait to get started, well now it's my turn with Noah. I have been waiting for this since he was born, since we found out we were having a boy, and I want to do it my way."

"Yes but that wasn't dangerous was it!" Noah tried to imagine what they were talking about, but he couldn't he was too confused.

"No one told me, my father didn't say anything until I confided in him about what was happening to me, and that was only after I started to notice his strange behaviour." His mother didn't reply. He just heard his mother putting clean pans and cups back in the cupboard. Noah was considering entering the kitchen and demanding they tell him what they were talking about.

Since when do you eavesdrop?" Roxy whispered in his ear. She startled him, he hadn't heard her creeping up behind him. He'd pushed the door open slightly when he'd jumped. Greg opened the door to find Noah stood there and Roxy behind him. Roxy pushed passed him into the kitchen.

"Noah over heard you two talking about him," she said, as she took a glass out the cupboard and poured orange juice into it. Noah felt his heart race, he was going to deny it when anger and curiosity took over, and he spoke without thinking.

"What were you talking about?"

"Nothing doesn't matter," Anne quickly replied, avoiding looking her son.

"I don' believe you, it was about me!" he said, getting more frustrated.

"Just tell him, he's gonna find out soon anyway," Roxy said as she took a sip of her juice. Noah didn't know who he was madder at: Roxy because obviously she knew and never told him, or his parents.

"No, Roxy no one is telling him anything yet." She addressed her daughter with a serious tone. She turned to Noah. "I'm sorry."

"Why the hell not?" Roxy argued. "He overheard you talking, and he'll find out Sunday anyway, what difference does it make, if it was me I'd – " Roxy was interrupted by Greg.

"Leave us three alone a minute will you." Roxy took a breath and realised her father was serious.

"OK fine, but you don't know what it's like for him, with the nightmares and everything. If you hadn't made me promise not to tell him, I would have by now!" She made her way to the door, but before she went through it she turned to Noah, smiled and winked at him. Noah couldn't believe what just happened, she'd stood up for him for the first time in his life and was on his side. When she'd gone, Noah turned to face his parents.

"So you gonna tell me what's going on?" he asked. His father looked at him and was about speak, but his mother beat him to it.

"No!"

"But Anne…!"

"I mean it Greg!" Greg could tell his wife was serious, and meant it; he decided to agree with her. He huffed and, rubbed his forehead. He never thought he'd hear himself say what was coming.

"Your mother's right Noah, you'll find out soon enough." He looked at his son; he could tell he was more than just disappointed. "I'm sorry!" Noah lowered his head and nodded. He slowly walked out of the room, he thought that maybe they would change their minds, but they didn't. He wanted to go to his room to be alone. When he got the top of the stairs, he headed in the direction of his closed door.

"Hey, Noah," Roxy whispered. She had opened her door enough just to poke her head out; she was very secretive about her room. "Did they tell you?" Noah didn't turn around to answer he just shook his head, and pushed his door open.

I had a feeling they wouldn't, meet me downstairs at 12 mid-night."

"Why?" She had got his attention.

"Please Noah, just trust me…" She thought a moment, while looking directly at him into his eyes. "For once, please!"

"Alright, fine!" He went into his room, and lay on his bed. Something was going on something serious and he wanted to know what it was, he couldn't wait until Sunday, it was too far away. Then he thought of his plans with Jack and Lucy he was spending the afternoon with them. Deep in thought and tired he drifted off to sleep. The man from his previous dream appeared again, the room he was in was blurred, but as the man began to speak it slowly came into focus. It was an old room with little lighting; Noah guessed it was a dining room in a castle of some sort. There was a massive table in the centre with a big candlestick in the middle. Noah realised that was the only light in the room. There were five men sat at the table, two on each side and the man from before was at the head table as if he was a man of great importance. They were all dressed as though they lived a couple of centuries ago. Being very good at history, Noah thought late 17th early 18th century. The other four had the same image as their leader, only their hair was white, and their eyes were yellow. They were talking about some kind of gemstone. Noah couldn't work out why these men needed this gemstone, as some things they said were muted. Once or twice they made a reference to a kind of creature they were afraid of, and also to a particular myth or legend that they weren't entirely sure was just a story. Noah hadn't noticed the wine glasses that were on the table, one for each of the men, until one of them picked theirs up to take a sip of the crimson liquid that was in each. The liquid also seemed unusually thick for red wine, which was what Noah thought it was at first. Noah then heard a distant knocking; it took him a moment to realise someone was knocking on his bedroom door.

"Who is it?" he said in a sleepy voice, and also slightly slurred.

"It's me, it's almost 12 o'clock," Roxy replied as loud as she could, but she didn't want to wake her mother.

"Oh yeah, right I'm up," he said standing up off his bed. He was still half asleep and as he walked to his door he found himself staggering. He joined Roxy on the landing and followed close behind her as they crept down the stairs. They heard their father leave out the door.

"What are we doing?" Noah whispered, as the headlights of Greg's car illuminated the hallway.

"Following Dad!" Roxy replied as she grabbed her keys and went towards the door. As Greg eased out of the driveway she opened the door.

"Why?" Noah remained stood on the stairs.

"Just come on otherwise we'll never find where it is." She stepped outside and jogged towards her car; she immediately climbed in the driver's side. Noah followed seating himself in the passenger's side.

"Find the way to where?"

"You'll see." As she spoke she smiled at him. She drove slowly along the road a distance away from Greg's car; she hadn't switched on her headlights. It seemed obvious she couldn't let their father notice they were following him. Noah had decided to tell Roxy all about the dream he'd just had.

"That's strange who were they?" she asked, not taking her eyes off Greg's car as he took a left passed Sanford Lake.

"I don't know." He glanced out the window and turned back to continue.

"They were talking about some kind of gemstone, and mentioned some sort of creature they were afraid of, it didn't make much sense." He also told her about the crimson liquid they were drinking, and that he didn't think it was red wine.

"Maybe it was blood," she suggested. She put her foot on the brake as she noticed their father park his car.

"That's crazy, are you telling me I'm dreaming about vampires." Roxy switched off the ignition and began to open her door.

"Come on we're going to follow Dad, but you have to be very quiet." She slid out of the car and shut the door quietly. Noah copied her. They ran to edge of Sanford Wood. Roxy looked deep into the trees, she could see the silhouette of her father in the dark. He was far enough away that they could enter. She gestured to Noah for him to follow her as she crept though the trees. They stopped at points and hid behind trees. Eventually they followed Greg to a clearing, at the opposite side there was an entrance to what looked like a cave. Greg entered. Roxy and Noah followed, as they walked slowly through the entrance they could hear voices.

"What is this place?" Noah asked, Roxy didn't reply. "Why's Dad here?"

"Shhhh, we have to be very q…quiet." Noah nodded, but he couldn't resist asking just one more question. "Why did you bring me here?" he said grabbing her arm. She spun round to answer him.

"I promised Mum and Dad I wouldn't tell you, they said nothing about showing you."

"Show me what?"

"Look would you please shut up, they can't know we're here."

"Who's they, it's Dad!"

"Noah!"

"Alright, I'll zip it." Roxy seemed to be looking for a passage, and also panicking.

"Oh god where is it!" she said as she got more and more agitated. Noah daren't speak, he just left her to it. He had no idea what was going on or why, which at this point to Roxy was a bad thing. Eventually she found the passage she was looking for; she gestured to Noah to follow her, but he just stood looking at her. Noah's claustrophobic and won't even get into a lift, never mind a small narrow passage way in a cave.

"Don't be a baby, it's safer in there than out here trust me."

"How is that even possible?" Roxy just shrugged her shoulders and climbed in. As her feet disappeared Noah got up his courage to go in after her. He looked into the passage; it was very dark and damp. Noah took a deep breath and climbed in. He had to crawl on his hands and knees; he could feel his heart pounding against his chest. Roxy was now in some kind of chamber area, and he could see a dim light.

"Come on." Roxy was getting annoyed at Noah. She secretly thought he was a wimp for being claustrophobic, and always teased him about it. Finally he joined his sister in the chamber, she had her back to him and was looking though a peephole. Noah could only hear voices.

"I'm sorry Caleb, my wife insisted I didn't tell him or bring him tonight." He could tell that was his father's voice, it was the others he didn't recognise.

"It's alright Greg, we have things to take care of anyway." The man that speaking was quiet a moment then he spoke again.

"They're back, and they are getting more and more comfortable, we need to shake their confidence." Just as he finished some more men arrived.

"Are we ready to go?" He thought he heard Joel's voice.

"Roxy, was that Joel?" he asked, she didn't reply she just nodded.

Two men argued whether Joel and his friends should join them. One made the point that they didn't have the experience, and another that they needed their youth and strength.

"Alright, they can join us, but no messing around, this is serious," said Caleb, who Noah could tell must be the leader.

"Oh yes, we finally get to fight vampires," Tyler said excitedly. Noah froze, he didn't speak or move. He couldn't believe what he'd just heard. Roxy turned and looked at him.

"That's right," she said. She looked back into the peephole, and then pulled back.

"Go on look." She pointed to the small hole in the cave wall. Noah approached slowly and with caution, when he reached the hole he hesitated. After a moment, he decided that there was something that Roxy really wanted him to see. And as no one else would let him in on it, he decided to trust her. He looked in the hole. He saw his father, and a man he suspected was Caleb. There were four other older men, Joel and his gang, all of them were stood in a circle. None were speaking or chanting, they just had their eyes closed, with their arms out slightly away from their bodies.

"What are they doing, is Dad apart of some kind of cult?" he asked.

"Just watch, please!" He continued to watch, as they started to get a bit taller, and hair began to sweep over and cover their bodies, their clothes started to rip. Noah gasped. And as he did, he saw ears point up on the top of their heads, their jaws started to get longer and a row of very shape teeth also began to appear. Noah kept his eyes on what he thought was his father, but he wasn't sure. They all more or less looked the same: they looked like big giant wolves.

"That's it; Dad is a werewolf..." She paused; as she did Noah turned and looked deep in her eyes. He knew what was coming, he knew what she was she was going to say next.

"You are a... You are a werewolf." She confirmed it. Even though he could not deny what he had just seen, he didn't believe it, it didn't make sense, it wasn't possible.

"Be very quiet, until they leave," she whispered. "We are safe in here."

Not only was Noah quiet he was also very still, he daren't move. He was in shock, scared and to his surprise a bit excited. He'd always thought that he was a normal boy, and a geek, but this was cool; he thought about what Lucy and Jack would think. Maybe Lucy might fall for him the way he's fallen for her. They were still and quiet for what seemed like an eternity.

"We have to take care from here on, we don't know how far away they are. I can try to do a spell, but Mum has only shown me, I've never actually tried it." When she looked at him she could tell his thoughts were miles away. She waved her hand in his face, and clicked her fingers to get his attention.

"What spell, what are you talking about?" he finally said. "Wait are you and Mum!"

Another surprise he thought.

"Witches!" She finished his sentence, but she seemed confused at his surprise.

29

"Sorry Mum did say she was going to tell you about that soon, before the weekend."

"Well she clearly forgot." Noah walked towards the entrance they'd crawled through.

"Yeah, something is going on, I've never known Mum, Dad and everyone act so strange." Noah said nothing, he thought she was joking and laughed. Then he saw the serious look on her face and realised, nothing about any of this was funny. He shrugged it off as being nervous laughter. They still had to walk all the through the woods back to the car, with werewolves and vampires in the surrounding area. And as they were making their way back outside, Roxy told him that werewolves and vampires alike have an incredible sense of smell. She was also quick to point out that the werewolves in Sanford protected humans from vampires, so they may not be the problem, but they still needed to be cautious. They made it to the middle of the woods without any confrontation; they were half way there. Both Noah and Roxy stopped in their tracks, they heard rustling to the left of them. Their breathing was slow but heavy with fear. They'd worked out that the wolf pack, as they were known, had gone in the opposite direction. So vampires were what was on Roxy's mind. The rustling had stopped for a few minutes.

"Noah, run!" Roxy said as she started to run herself, Noah followed closely behind. As they ran they heard something chasing them. Neither of them dared turn around. They made it to the car, Roxy fumbled in her bag for her keys, as she did she looked up, and saw a tall figure standing just outside the trees. She panicked and dropped her keys. She fumbled again and finally found them again, she gripped them tight determined not to drop them this time. As she put the key in the lock, the figure started to walk towards them. Noah started pulling on the handle, in a fit of panic. Roxy turned the key and they jumped in. The figure picked up its pace, as it got closer, both Roxy and Noah pushed the locks down on their doors. When Noah looked up the figure had gone.

"It's gone, I think!" he said turning to look at Roxy.

"Don't be too sure!" she replied. Just then there was a bang on the roof." She confirmed it. Even though he could not deny what he had heard. "Told ya!" she said smiling and starting the ignition. She instantly put the car into gear, and they shot forwards, whatever was on the roof had fallen onto the gravel. Noah turned to look back.

"I think you hurt him!" Noah yelled. Roxy turned the car round. As she did Noah kept his eyes on the figure on the ground. He saw it stand up straight and face the car. The headlights shone a beam of light on and around the figure. She sped forwards, towards it and just before it jumped up out of the way, Noah caught a glimpse of his face. It looked familiar, but he couldn't place him in all the excitement and panic.

They drove back home, both of them remaining silent the entire journey, until they parked up on the driveway. They noticed that the landing and living room lights were on, and that meant one thing, their mother was up and she was waiting for them.

"I can't do anything, without her finding out!" Roxy paused, shook her head and huffed. "And this is without magic!" she continued.

"It's what mums do, let's go in and face the music, I'm tired," Noah said, opening the car door.

Roxy grabbed Noah's arm. "We'll sneak in." She opened her car door slightly and edged out gently. Noah just got out of the car. And stood up straight.

"Will you get down she might see!" Roxy said keeping close to the ground.

"She knows we're out here!" he said walking behind her and laughing.

"I have a way in without her knowing!"

"How?" Noah asked, although he had a feeling he didn't want to know. Roxy was enjoying herself she loved being a rebel, sneaking into the house late at night when she wasn't supposed to be out was her specialty at the moment.

"Get down or she might see you!" Roxy said creeping around the front of the car on her hands and knees. Noah repeated that their mother knew they were out there.

"Maybe not, she's a light sleeper, and always gets up for a coffee, or a vodka!" With that Noah quickly joined Roxy on the floor. "What's the plan then Bond?" Roxy looked at him with a blank expression. "You know as in James Bond, we're sneaking in!" he continued.

"Yes I know what you meant, follow me and stay low!" She crept to the side of the house, and round the back, remaining the whole time on her hands and knees. Noah followed close behind. When they were both in the back garden, she stood up. Noah copied her. Roxy pointed to a small window that was almost level with the ground. "I always prop the cellar window open a bit, easy access!" Noah at this moment thought he'd not given Roxy enough credit, she was an evil genius, he'd have never have thought of that. They walked over to the window. Roxy carefully opened it more and edged her way through, slowly. When she was in the cellar and there was no sign of movement above her she signalled to Noah to join her. As he was edging his way in, Roxy was getting a box out of a dark corner. She pulled out two dressing gowns. One was a deep pink and the other was navy.

"Here put this on over your clothes, and take off your shoes." She passed him the navy one. He did as she said and he handed her his shoes, while she put on the pink one. She placed their shoes in the box, and got out a bottle of water, she dapped some drops on her hand, and proceeded to lightly wet her eyes. As she did it smudged her mascara. She then put her hands on her hair and slightly messed it up; Noah did the same with his.

"Why are we doing all this?" he whispered.

"Just in case she sees us, we can say we snuck down for a drink. I do it all the time; well sometimes I actually do come down for a drink and let her see me coming down the stairs. So when I do sneak in it's more believable!"

"I don't give you enough credit; you're a genius on the sly!"

"Yeah well, keep it to yourself I have a reputation." She smiled at him, and Noah felt as though they were bonding. He'd never really seen this side of her before. She was being nice, and smiling, and he knew she was enjoying herself. They began to creep up the stairs to the kitchen. Roxy opened the door to enter, she looked around, the coast was clear. She proceeded to walk in, and Noah followed close behind. They could just about hear the television in the living room, an indication their mother was up. They ascended up the stairs, as quietly as they could, there was no indication Anne had heard them. Noah went straight to his room and Roxy went to hers. As he lay on his bed, he tried to comprehend what he'd seen and what Roxy had told him. When he woke up that morning, everything was normal, and he had no idea these things existed. He wondered how he'd not noticed all these years, how can they all live in secret? As he mulled it over he fell asleep, he hadn't bothered to get ready for bed, or get under the covers.

Three

Noah woke suddenly. He thought at first it was one of nightmares that had woken him, but he couldn't recall having one and he usually remembered them. It was Saturday the day before his birthday, before his turning. He sat on his bed, he didn't want to face his father. He didn't know how to act, and somehow he knew his father saw him, or sensed his presence last night. He heard Roxy get up and go downstairs. He thought for a moment and decided to go down himself.

His parents were in the kitchen. Roxy had gone into the living room, he was just about to turn and leave when his father spoke. "Sleep well last night?" he asked, there was something about his tone that convinced Noah even more that he knew.

"Erm… Yeah I did thanks!" Noah replied. He'd never felt so uncomfortable in all his life. How do you act around your father when you discover he's a werewolf? At that moment his father winked at him. Noah turned and opened the door to leave. "Go get dressed, we're going fishing, like we used to!" his father said as Noah walked through the door, he just nodded back, and went to his room. He looked in his wardrobe and tried to find something suitable to wear. Then he wondered if his father was really taking him, or if it was a decoy to fool his mother. He couldn't think straight, he felt himself feeling paranoid, and didn't like it. He decided eventually to dress for fishing. Greg did enjoy fishing. The two of them used go all the time, and it had been years since their last trip.

When he was finally ready, he met Greg in the garage. He was digging out all their old fishing gear. "So where are we going?" Noah asked.

"Sanford Lake, the spot we always used to go to," Greg replied. "We need to talk father to son!" Noah helped him load everything into the boot of the car. They said goodbye to Anne, who'd been standing at the door watching them.

They drove in silence, Noah daren't speak, he'd had the thought of telling all morning he and Roxy had followed him, but if he had known surly he would tell him, maybe that was what he wanted to talk about, Noah thought. Greg parked the car. Noah grabbed his fishing rod and tackle from the boot. They took the path that led to a little beach on the bank of the lake, they cast their lines propped them up and waited for a bite. They remained quiet for a while, both just staring out at the lake. Greg was the first to break the silence.

"I know you followed me last night, my sense of smell is great you know." He paused for a moment, but before Noah could speak Greg continued. "It was stupid and reckless, but in way I'm glad you did, saves me the trouble of telling you who you really are. Don't tell your mother, she'll have kittens, night-time is dangerous around here."

"I know, me and Roxy saw a vampire!" Noah said. He regretted it, he thought his Father would lecture him about following instead of being laid back about it.

"So you know they exist too then, good, get used to seeing them, after tomorrow that will become a regular thing!" Greg continued. "One thing I have to tell you, and be very clear on this, you can't tell anyone, not even Jack or Lucy, they will just

35

think you've gone insane. That may not be as hard as you think, because as of Monday, you can't hang around with them any more."

"What!" He thought for a minute. He wanted to challenge his Father on this and chose his argument carefully. "Won't that make them suspicious of something?"

"Probably, but that's the way it is, we have these rules for a reason, and breaking one under any circumstances comes with a harsh price!"

"They've been my friends all my life, I can't just cut them out of it, just like that!"

"I'm sorry, but you have to Noah!" Greg didn't look at him, he knew hearing this hurt him, he didn't want to see that look on his face.

"Just explain to me why!" Noah looked at Greg and tried to get him to look back, Greg eventually gave in, he wanted Noah to realise how important and necessary it was.

"Humans in this town live in peace, they go about their lives fearless, if they knew it wouldn't be that way. We protect them from vampires, no werewolf in this town has ever attacked a human. Also there would be danger for us too, they would try to hunt us, drive us away, making them sitting ducks for vampires, and we can't do that!" When Greg had spoken he turned back to look at the lake.

"OK, I understand, we're the good guys right!" Greg just nodded and smiled.

"What about if they see us though?" Noah asked.

"They don't, see us, and the only humans that see vampires become their prey!"

"So vampires only drink human blood?"

"Yes, unfortunately, sometimes they bite to turn them, to up their numbers. That's happened recently, we're not sure

36

who though just yet, but if you get close enough to a human who will soon turn, you can smell it on them!" Noah couldn't think of any more questions. Just then he noticed he'd got a fish that was tugging on his line. He grabbed a hold of his rod and with all his strength, he began to reel it in. He could tell already that it was a trout. And when he'd got it on the beach that was confirmed. He hit it over the head and placed its corpse into the box.

"Present for Mum, I know she likes trout!" Greg smiled at him in a proud way. He put another bait on his line and cast it out again. He decided to tell his father about his dreams; Noah thought maybe he could make some sense of them. When he'd finished telling him all the details Greg spoke.

"I don't what they mean, when you meet Caleb, tell him, he's the pack leader and oldest of all of us!" Greg answered. "He will be interested, I don't think that's ever occurred before!" Noah was a little worried at that thought. He'd already found out that he was different, he didn't want to be unique and unusual in the werewolf world, he wanted to fit in with them that was all. They fished for a while longer, but didn't catch anything else. It was starting to come dark, so they set off back to the car.

It was on the way home that Noah realised that this was the beginning of a new life for him, and tomorrow would be the last day he would spend with his two best friends. He tried not to think of that. He tried to focus on the fact that he would be contributing to their safety, which made him smile, until he remembered that they would never know that, they would think that he had abandoned them completely without reason. Somehow he knew he'd have to put the thought to the back of his mind and not dwell on it, it would just make what's to come even harder for him. He also realised that people can never have everything. He was closer to his sister like he wanted, Joel and the others would no longer give him grief as he will be joining their gang, but he has to sacrifice his friendship with two people who have always liked him and stood by him no matter what. There was nothing he could do about it; he'd tried to think of a way he could tell them without anyone knowing, if that was possible. He imagined what would happen if he did, only to discover that his father was right, nothing good would come of it, and they probably wouldn't believe him.

When he got home he had his dinner with his family. They ate in silence which was strange. When Noah had finished he went for a shower, then into his room where he remained for the rest of night. He wanted to be alone. He checked his mobile phone for any messages from Lucy or Jack, but there weren't any, which he thought was strange. When they weren't together they always texted each other, three-way messaging as they called it. They sent every message to each other, so basically, they sent every message twice, it cost more, but that's what they did. He decided to send them both a message, just to see how their day had gone. He didn't get a reply from either of them. He switched on his television. As he watched the news he began to feel his eyes close, he tried to keep awake, but it was no use. So eventually he gave in, as he did he heard a knock on his door, it was Roxy. Even though he'd told her to go away, she opened the door and waltzed in.

"Dad told me and Mum he spoke with you on your fishing trip, how you feeling?" she said sitting on his bed. He replied with a grunt.

"Don't get mad, but I bumped into Lucy today."

"Why would I get mad?" He paused and thought about what Roxy could be like. "What did you say to her?" He sat up and was almost fully awake again.

"Nothing really!" She looked at floor as she replied.

"Roxy!"

"It was her OK, if you must know, she said that I should be more sensitive to your feelings, and try to be there for you in your time of need, and to stop telling Joel and the others about your business!"

"She's not wrong!" he said in a slightly angry tone. He knew what was coming next, he knew that there was no way that Roxy would keep her cool, she hated Lucy, for reasons unknown to him.

"I may have said something out of context!" He was right; he smiled and nodded in way of confirming with himself.

"What did you say?"

"That as of Monday your business isn't going to concern her or Jack, and also to come terms with the fact you won't be friends any more!" Not only did she avoid eye contact with Noah, she avoided looking at him at all.

"Why did you say that?"

"Well it's true isn't it!"

"It wasn't your place to tell her though was it?" He paused and then continued. "Tomorrow I was supposed to go bowling with them, which would have been a nice seeing as though that won't happen again, and you've gone and ruined it!" He stood up and moved towards the window.

"I'm sorry, I know I was wrong!"

"That's not good enough, you never think about other people's feelings and who you hurt... Just leave I don't want to talk to you or look at you!" He had his back turned to her; she got up and moved towards him, he just shrugged her away.

"I'll fix it, I promise!"

"How, what's the point, it is true, for once you actually told the truth!"

"Exactly I'll tell her it was a wind up, that I just wanted to upset her and make her mad." With that she grabbed Noah's mobile to find Lucy's number, when she had found it she began to put it into her phone, then proceeded to text her. Noah remained silent and kept his back to her. When she'd finished she put mobile back into her pocket, moments later her phone rang. Noah could hear Roxy trying to explain to Lucy what was apparently going on. He thought it was no use. After ten minutes Roxy hung up.

"It worked you're back on for tomorrow!" She paused and made her way back to the door. "Alright well I'll leave you alone now!" She closed the door behind her, Noah went and sat back on his bed, he put his head on his pillow for a second and fell back asleep.

Four

Noah sat up on his bed, he rubbed eyes. He'd had another strange dream, this time his English teacher, Mr Fisher, was there with the vampires. He didn't understand why? He looked at his mobile phone, he'd got a message from Lucy telling him to meet her and Jack at 2 p.m. He looked at the time, it was nearly 11 a.m., he'd slept in. he wondered why no one had woke him for breakfast.

"Can I come in?" He heard Roxy on the other side of the door. He was still mad at her, but it was his birthday, so he thought he should be nice and try to keep the peace.

"Alright!" he replied. She opened the door and strolled in, she was carrying a package. She held it out for him grab, but he didn't make any attempt to do so, so she placed it on his bed.

"Happy Birthday!" She smiled as she sat on the end of his bed. He just looked at it and then back at her.

"Aren't you going to open it?" she asked. He huffed and reached for it; at first he shook it and whatever was inside rattled around in the box. He then proceeded to tear off the paper; in his hands was now a white box. He opened it to find there was a medallion inside. He looked at her.

"It's the werewolf medallion, they all have one, given to them on their 17th Birthday, I wanted to give you yours." He put it round his neck, got up to look in the mirror. As he did he noticed he was a bit taller, when he was opening his present he hadn't noticed his biceps and forearms were slightly bigger too. He pulled up his top to see he almost had a six pack.

"That's just the beginning, they will be bigger tomorrow!" He smiled at her. The medallion suited him. "Now you've put it on, you have to wear it all the time, you must never take it off!" Roxy said.

"Why?" he asked.

"Don't know, you just can't!" With that she left. He began to get dressed, he felt the need to style his hair nice. He went to the bathroom, and picked up the tub of hair gel he hadn't used in a while, and began rubbing it in his hair, and spiked it up. When he was done he looked in the mirror, and smiled at himself, for first time he liked his appearance.

When he got downstairs his parents immediately handed him his gift from them. It was a book.

"It will help you, it may answer some questions," Greg said to him. The book's title read 'WEREWOLF BOOK OF HISTORY, RULES AND LAWS'.

"Thanks!" Noah replied, studying the cover, and flipping through the pages. Anne went to the kitchen. When she returned she was carrying a chocolate cake, with a 17 candle on the top. His family sang happy birthday to him. She put the cake down on the coffee table in the centre of the room. She cut four equal pieces from it, and passed them round.

When Noah was finished he looked at the clock, and realised he had to be at Lucy's house in twenty minutes.

"I've got to meet Lucy and Jack now!" He stood up and headed for the door, he turned and smiled at his family, thanked them then left.

He hadn't walked far down the road when he bumped into Lucy and Jack. They hardly recognised him.

"Mate, what happened to you?" Jack asked, looking slightly shocked.

"Nothing why?" Noah replied.

"Your body... you look different!" Lucy added.

"Oh that, just been lifting some weights with my dad that's all!" Both Jack and Lucy looked at him with disbelief. "Nice to know it's paid off!" Noah said as he started walking down the street, Jack and Lucy followed.

As they walked, both Lucy and Jack put Noah's new appearance to the back of their minds. Noah couldn't help thinking that this would be the last time he would ever really chat with them. Jack started talking about Joel.

"What's with Joel, I mean he's so arrogant, I don't think I've ever seen him in a good mood!"

"Maybe he's misunderstood!" Noah replied without thinking. He looked at them and continued, "I mean we don't know him, he might have problems, you know at home or something!"

"What, Noah, Joel has been tormenting you for years why all of a sudden are you defending him?" Jack said. He looked slightly furious at Noah's outburst.

"No reason, sometimes things like that can make people act that way, you never really know what's going on inside people... I mean people's minds," Noah added.

"I don't care what you think, I have problems at home and I don't act that way, so that's no excuse," Lucy butted in.

"Yeah I suppose you're right.... Don't know why I said it." Noah pretended to look confused at his own outburst, and as they walked he started to get slightly nervous. He's not good at fooling people, especially Lucy who can tell when he's lying or hiding something. He barely spoke another word, until they reached the bowling alley. They opened the big blue double doors, and paid to get in. Noah looked around, it had changed since he was last there, which had been years. There were extra lanes, a nice little café area, and also a bar. In the entrance area there were a few arcade games, pool table and also an air hockey table, behind that was the kiosk were they got their bowling shoes.

"It's changed a bit since I was last here!" Noah said. Jack and Lucy just smiled at each other. They walked towards the kiosk. Jack spoke to the man, he didn't say much just confirmed their booking. He took their shoes off the counter and replaced them with red and white bowling shoes. Lucy pulled a disgusted face as she slipped them on. She couldn't help but think of the countless sweaty feet that had been in them before her. They made their way towards the bar and ordered some drinks and three baskets of fries. Jack and Lucy insisted it was their treat and split the cost. They picked a lane and began their game. Noah went first, he bowled a strike, Jack got a spare and Lucy only knocked down a few pins on her first throw and four others on her second throw. She claimed she had to get warmed up first, Jack and Noah just laughed at her.

They played a few games, Noah won two games and Jack won the other. They didn't want to leave straight away so they decided to play some pool and air hockey. They took turns at playing each other. Pool was Jack's game, no one could ever beat him, and to Noah and Jack's surprise Lucy shined at air hockey. So the wins for the day, in their eyes were equal.

When they set off home it was 8 p.m. and already getting dark, and as Noah was now aware of what lurked around at night he insisted that they didn't hang around. It was dark by the time they reached the bottom of blossom drive, where Jack lived and parted ways.

"See you two tomorrow at school!" Jack said.

"Yeah!" There was a hint of uncertainty in his voice that Lucy picked up on.

"Don't sound too excited!" Jack said as he walked off. "Didn't know I was that bad to look at." Noah could tell Jack was joking but he didn't laugh or say anything, he just half smiled, in fact he didn't even look at Jack, he just looked at the floor. He thought if he made eye contact with Jack he'd figure it out.

"I'll walk you home!" Noah said to Lucy.

"That's OK. It's not that far," she replied

"I insist, you don't know what's walking around at night." She looked at him with a confused expression. "I mean who's walking around at night... who!"

"What, you think there are dangerous people in little Sanford... We know everyone who lives here!" She giggled and walked ahead. He caught up with her and grabbed her arm.

"Just humour me, please."

"Alright fine," she replied. She looked at him as if he was stupid or insane, but she gave him the benefit of the doubt when she saw how serious he was. They didn't talk much, Noah was constantly scanning the area, he'd never felt so alert before. He realised what he was doing and wondered if it had started already. So he insisted that they walked faster.

Finally they made it to Lucy's house, Noah was glad that they hadn't come across anything. They said good night and Lucy was just about to walk up the path, when Noah grabbed her arm. As she turned her head Noah leaned in and kissed her. She didn't push him away, she found herself kissing him back, she realised what she was doing and pulled away.

"What are you doing?" she asked, trying to catch his gaze at the same time. She freed her arm from his grip. "Noah, answer me!" she demanded.

He didn't look at her at first. But, without thinking, he replied, "I love you… I've always loved you!" He paused, waiting for her to say something or a reaction, when he got neither from her he continued. "I don't care if you don't feel the same, actually I don't want you to tell me, I just want you to know how I feel… Sorry about the kiss." He turned to walk away, as he did he felt intense heat creep into his body. He wasn't sure if it was nerves or something else, he just knew that he'd never felt like this before. He didn't want to find out with Lucy close behind him to witness it. As he sped up the heat spread more and more, until his whole body was reaching what he thought must be boiling point, and then a tingling sensation began in his muscles. Lucy shouted after him.

"NOAH, NOAH! YOU CAN'T JUST WALK AWAY!" She started running after him, he heard her footsteps on the pavement, and with that increased his pace. As he ran he glanced up at the sky, a full moon. He could hear Lucy was still behind him, she was a fast runner, and she was on the running team for school. Goosebumps now started to appear on his arms, and as he glanced down, he saw the hairs on his arms get longer, he could feel the hairs all over his body were doing the same. He also began to feel a piercing sensation in his fingertips and especially in his gums. He touched his teeth and felt fangs and also noticed he had claws.

He quickly turned a corner, and ran as fast as he could down a dark alley. Where he was suddenly met by a dead end. A seven foot wall stood in his way. He leaned up against it, and let out a scream of pain as his jaw changed shaped, from that of a human to something that more resembled a wolf. His muscles ached as they began to get bigger. The lower part of his legs started to bend the other way. He let out another scream, although this time it was more like a howl. He could still hear Lucy in the distance, he fell to the floor, and to his surprise he started to turn back to normal. When he was fully normal again he laid on the floor flat on his back. After a while he stood back up. He still felt strange, and he wobbled a bit before he found his feet, and his head felt heavy. He took a couple of steps, and then stopped, he bent over, put his hands on his knees and threw up. He stood up straight and wiped his mouth. His heart was beating fast against his ribcage.

He walked slowly towards the entrance to alley, and found Lucy was still there. She noticed him stood under the beam of the streetlight, and bolted towards him.

"What was all that about?" she asked in an angry tone.

"I'm sorry I panicked!" he replied.

"You can't just...." She stopped as she looked at his chest. "What's that?" she asked, moving closer for a better look at his medallion. He looked down and noticed that it was in clear view.

"Oh this?" he said, as he gripped it in his hand. "Roxy gave it to me for my birthday!"

"It looks like the one Joel and the others wear...." She paused and thought for a moment. "Is that why you defended him earlier?" He shook his head.

"I don't believe you!" she said enraged. "Roxy was right!"

"What?" he asked, pretending to be confused.

"Doesn't matter, you've changed, I don't know how or why, but you're not the same person you was on Friday!" Tears started to fill her eyes and roll down her cheeks. Noah just looked at her. She turned and walked away. Noah had never made her cry before, and she felt as though she couldn't be around him. He went after her he just watched as she turned the corner, she didn't look back like he'd hoped.

He set off home. When he got there, he just went straight to his room. He slammed his door, and hit it with his fist, to his surprise it didn't hurt. He saw the book his mother and father had given him earlier, he picked it up, and flicked through it to see if it mentioned anything about turning. He had no luck so he put it down on his desk. It was obvious to him that what had happened earlier was a turning as his father put it.

He undressed and got into bed. He fell straight to sleep, but it wasn't a restful sleep, he tossed and turned, sweat was pouring off him. Until eventually he settled properly.

Five

As the night fell and everyone in town was settling down to the evening television or going to bed, up on the hillside just outside Sanford was a castle. And they were just waking up. Drake stood on the balcony looking down towards the town; he was working out their next move. Sebastian came to join him.

"There are werewolves in this area!" said Sebastian, as he walked to join Drake, when he reached his side he continued, "They are making it hard for us to hunt!" Drake could tell by the look on his face Sebastian wasn't happy.

"I knew that before we arrived, I've been here before about a hundred years ago!" Drake replied.

"Then why did you lead us here?" Sebastian was slightly enraged by Drake's confession, he stood facing his leader. Drake didn't answer straight away, he just stared into the dark night, and then he glanced at the moon, it was bright. The brightest it had been for some time; Drake knew what that meant, another werewolf turning had occurred.

"I'm here for revenge, on a certain werewolf..." Drake paused to see if Sebastian knew what he talking about, then continued. "The one that killed my father!" He got little response from Sebastian on the matter, instead he changed the subject.

"What about our hunting?" Sebastian asked. "We are running out of fresh blood, my Lord, the others are getting very anxious!"

"So long as we keep a low profile we should be fine!" Drake started to walk back inside. "I heard that someone has bit a human in order to turn him?" Drake sounded very concerned by this.

"Yes, Dorian did!" Sebastian could tell Drake wanted a reason. "If we are going to take on the werewolves we need to up our numbers!"

"I know, but that's not keeping a low profile though is it. Werewolves can smell it on people when they have been bitten for a change, and then when that person comes looking for us, they follow!" Sebastian felt ashamed, that he had let his leader down. They remained quiet for some time. Drake broke the silence.

"Before my Father died he bit this werewolf!" Sebastian listened intently. It was common knowledge to the vampires that a single bite couldn't kill a werewolf – just make him very ill.

"I should continue this at the meeting, you all need to know!" Drake started to descend the stairs just outside his door, Sebastian followed.

When he entered the dining room, the others were already seated. Anyone could tell who the leader was. Drake had long dark hair that reached past his shoulders, and his eyes were bright red. The others also had long hair the same length as Drake's but theirs was white, and they had bright yellow eyes. Drake made his way to his usual seat at the head of the table. Each of them had a glass of blood; this was how the elders made decisions. Drake started by telling what he'd told Sebastian.

"Taking revenge and claiming this town back won't be easy!" Drake said.

"You're right about that, have you ever killed a werewolf?" Dorian interrupted, as he took a sip of blood.

"There are ways in which it can be done!" Carlos added. "I've seen it!"

"Excellent!" Drake replied. "To make it easier my father told me about a gemstone, created by the witches on our side, and when they have done their ritual with it, we will be able to walk in the daylight!" Again it was common knowledge to vampires that werewolves could only turn at night, during the day, no matter what they remained in human form.

"So where is this gemstone located?" asked Isaac.

"Hidden by the witches of Sanford, Giselle and the other witches are going to infiltrate their cavern, in order to discover its true location!"

"As I mentioned before my father bit the werewolf that attacked him, as you know it didn't kill him, but it will have affected his son, who as you know will also be a werewolf!"

"So, what does that matter?" Dorian said, laughing slightly.

"He will be the strongest werewolf of this time. It's been three hundred years since an occurrence, he will be impossible to kill, and if Logan and his pack of dogs work this out and get wind of our plan, this boy is all they'll need to finish us all off!"

"Yes but he's just an inexperienced puppy!" they all laughed. Vampires liked to refer to werewolves as dogs, and the younger ones as puppies, it was their way of hiding the fact that they were really scared of them, and that werewolves were stronger than they were. The only advantage a vampire had against a werewolf was that they can fly. If they could get a good tight grip on a werewolf, they could lift them hundreds of feet into air, and then let go, hurtling the werewolf to the ground, and from that height they wouldn't land on their feet. This was hard for vampires to do, as werewolves had an incredible attacking speed. More vampires ended up being torn to pieces than werewolves being dropped from great heights. Drake summoned the witches into the room. Giselle strolled in first, with her hair brown and looked as though it hadn't been brushed in weeks. She was the eldest of the four witches in the castle. She was accompanied by her two daughters, Crystal and Missy. Raven, the youngest, in fact she was only a teenager, was an orphan whom they took in when she was five years old. Drake went over the plan for them for the next day, but he'd added another part to it.

"Raven you are enrolled at the school, effective tomorrow," Drake said.

"What, why, what do I need to go to school for!" Raven said, she seemed furious at the concept.

"To befriend the young group of witches, and find out what they know!" Drake replied.

"How did you manage that?" Carlos asked.

"With thanks to a certain someone I have turned!" Dorian said with a grin on his face. He dismissed them, and they left. When they had gone Drake and others went back to their meeting. Drake spoke but kept his voice quiet.

"One of you find out where they keep their elixir, and replace it, if they fail us, it'll be their blood on the table!" The faces of the other vampires lit up.

"But for now we need them," said Sebastian. After Sebastian had spoken they all rose and left the room. They needed to go on the hunt. Searching the streets of Sanford for a poor lonely sole walking home in the dark, there's bound to be at least one there always is.

Six

Morning arrived like any other in little Sanford. But for Noah Monday morning marked the beginning of a new life. Noah had woken up an hour before his alarm rang, which was very unusual. He laid for at least twenty minutes just staring at the ceiling trying to work out exactly how he felt. Part of him felt sad and also angry, because he couldn't speak to Jack or Lucy at school, the other part of him felt excited and also curious about all that was to come.

He'd had a good night sleep, for the first time in weeks; it wasn't interrupted by nightmares or bizarre dreams. Although he was still eager to find out what they meant, and when it comes to finally meet Caleb he would ask him if he knew what they meant.

He couldn't wait any longer, he jumped out of bed, as he did he could hear Roxy, going into the bathroom for her usual morning shower. He giggled to himself as she started to sing, as he strolled casually towards his wardrobe. He browsed the contents carefully, he wanted to look good on the first day of his new life, and also wanted to fit in with Joel and his friends. He found a nice pair of jeans that Roxy had bought him for Christmas, but couldn't find a T-shirt or shirt he thought would be a good match. He waited for Roxy to finish her shower, and immediately asked for her advice as soon as she appeared on the landing. She agreed to help him, and proceeded to follow him into his room. She looked at the T-shirts and shirts in his wardrobe, she didn't say anything but looked at him with complete hopelessness.

"Isn't there anything at all that looks cool?" he asked in desperation. Roxy reached far into the back, she pulled out a black T-shirt.

"This will do!" she said holding it up to Noah. He looked at it and smiled. He pulled it over his head, it was a tight fit, but that's what he wanted, as that was the style of Joel and the others.

"Thank god you bought me clothes for Christmas!" he said as he looked at himself in the mirror.

"I knew this day would come, and you'd have nothing cool to wear!" With that she left his room, and went to her own.

When Noah was dressed he went in the bathroom to style his hair, he decided on the spiky wet look. As he left his room he glanced at his bedside clock, and realised he didn't have enough time for breakfast. He could hear Roxy by the door getting her coat and shoes on.

"Noah hurry up, we need to meet the others!" she shouted up the stairs. With that he hurried downstairs.

"We'd better go then!" he replied, and followed her out of the door, to her car. They both got in. Roxy pulled out of the drive and drove down the street.

When they arrived at school, Noah was surprised to see Lucy waiting for him as she always did, considering the events of the night before. As he got out the car and walked up towards school with Roxy, he avoided looking at her. He knew she'd obviously seen him.

"Noah!" Lucy shouted. He ignored her, it was hard for him, but he knew it would make it a bit easier if he didn't look at her at all.

Joel and the others were waiting at the entrance to school.

"Hey Noah, welcome to our club!" Tyler said, giving Noah a jab in the arm with his fist. Roxy's friends Beth, Lacy and Paige, joined them. All the witches dressed in a sort of code too, like rock chicks. Beth had long light brown hair, which today had curls in. Lacy had long blonde hair, but she preferred hers to be straight. Paige on the other hand had short hair dark brown hair, that didn't even reach her ears; she liked to style her hair spiky at the back with her side fringe perfectly straight. Beth smiled at Noah in an admiring way; Noah didn't seem to notice this at all. Roxy noticed that Lucy was approaching them.

"Come on gang let's go inside, little miss nosy is walking this way!" Roxy said gesturing with a little nod over her shoulder, the others apart from Noah, glanced at her in a disgusted way, especially Beth. They all turned and walked in to school. Roxy and Joel made sure Noah wasn't at the back, they didn't want Lucy getting too close to Noah, or Jack for that matter. Greg and the other werewolf elders had made that quite clear, Joel and Roxy had to keep a close watch on those too and try to make things as easy as they can be for Noah. Unfortunately neither of them was in the same classes as Noah, so before he headed in a different direction to them, they made sure he was reminded of why he couldn't associate with them, and also where to meet them at breaks and during lunch.

"You'll get through it, it's hard the first couple of days, but it will soon get easier. Once they realise nothing they do or say can get your full attention, they will give up!" Joel said, in an attempt to reassure him.

"Not Lucy and Jack, they don't give up easily!" Noah replied.

"If they keep at you and it doesn't start to get any better, let us witches know. We know some harmless potions and spells that may help!" Roxy added. They noticed they were late for class and parted ways.

"Good luck mate!" Joel said. Noah just turned around nodded his head and smiled. He'd missed tutorial, so he headed straight to his English lesson. Before he opened the door he could tell Mr Fisher had already started his lesson. He walked in and Mr Fisher paused for a moment and then spoke.

"Well, well nice of you to finally join us!" Noah ignored his comment and strolled passed him, as he did a horrible smell hit him, he turned and glanced at his teacher. Mr Fisher looked back at him, and as he did, Noah could sense a glimmer of fear in his eyes. He turned away and went to back of the classroom, and sat on the table nearest the back. Jack and Lucy were in their usual seats, they looked at Noah, and Jack was going speak but before he could Mr Fisher continued the lesson.

As the lesson went on Lucy and Jack looked round at Noah a few times, but he didn't really notice. When that failed Jack wrote a note and threw it on Noah's desk. He didn't read it, he just placed it on the floor under his desk. Noah didn't pay attention to the lesson, and when it came to copy what was written on the board, he drew pictures of moons and also crucifixes in his book. It went on for what seemed like forever, when finally the bell rang, the other all stood up among them were Jack and Lucy, but unlike the others they didn't leave. He eventually stood and walked to the front of the room.

"Noah, I'd like a word!" Mr Fisher said, he turned to Jack and Lucy stood in the door way. "In private, please!" Both of them left and shut the door behind them. Mr Fisher turned back to Noah, studied him for a while and then finally spoke.

"About your detention this evening!" He paused.

"What about it!" Noah said in a cocky tone, the first time he'd ever spoke that way before, and he liked it.

"You don't have one!" Mr Fisher gestured him to leave, as he did, Jack and Lucy were waiting on the right and Roxy and Joel on the left. He ignored Jack completely and went straight to the right.

"Guess who doesn't have detention any more!" Noah asked Roxy and Joel smiling.

"You!" said Joel. "That was obvious!"

"Where are the others?" Noah asked, looking around.

"Outside, let's go," Roxy said, as they started to walk Roxy asked Noah how it went. And they also knew Jack and Lucy were following close behind, even though neither of them turned around.

"OK, didn't speak, didn't look, better that way!" Noah replied. "There was one thing though, as soon as I walked in there was this horrible lingering smell!"

"Where did it seem to be coming from?" Joel asked, this was more his field than Roxy's.

"Around Mr Fisher's desk and he looked at me strange!"

"He was scared of you, this smell, was it like rotting flesh!"

"Yes, sort of!" Joel looked at Noah, then at Roxy.

"What's that mean?" Roxy asked, although feeling as though she didn't want to know the answer.

"It means we're going to have another vampire to deal with!" answered Joel.

"Oh yeah that must be the smell my dad told me about!" said Noah, Joel nodded.

"We have to tell the others, he could be a spy at the moment, working out who we are!" They hurried their pace outside. Straight ahead Noah noticed a few trees around a bench, the others were all gathered underneath. As soon as they reached them Joel told them about Mr Fisher. He didn't leave out that Noah was the one who'd discovered this, even though Joel told him what it was he'd smelled like, he let Noah take full credit.

"Well done mate!" Callum also congratulated Noah with a slap on the back. Noah loved it and gloated as much as he could, he couldn't believe he was part of the cool crowd. Nearly everyone at school had seen, and they all seemed to instantly fear him, all except Jack and Lucy, who were stood at the school entrance watching the display in front of them in disbelief.

"I don't get what's going on!" Jack said.

"Neither do I, but after we left you last night he was acting strange!" Lucy thought for moment.

"I swear I'm going to find out!" As she spoke she watched with shear jealousy as Lacy kissed Noah on the cheek, and whispered in his ear, and then they both giggled.

"Maybe he's always been friends with them, and as a prank was pretending to be friends with us!" Jack said. He always came out with ridiculous things when he or no one else could come up with a good explanation straight away.

"You're so stupid!" Lucy commented as the display of Noah with Lacy and others seemed to be too much for her to take. She turned her back to them and went back into the school; Jack hesitated, and then followed her. The bell rang shortly after they walked in the building. Roxy walked Noah to his next lesson.

"So, how do you like being part of my group of friends?" she asked him.

"Great!" he answered enthusiastically.

"They're not as bad as you thought, are they?"

"No they're nice!" Noah turned the corner to his Science lesson, while Roxy continued straight ahead to her History lesson. History was the only lesson she actually enjoyed, except when she learned about what happened to witches in medieval England, she and her friends found it barbaric for obvious reasons. As she entered the classroom Paige had saved her a seat next to her, their teacher Mrs West had not arrived yet. On the table in front of her Beth was talking to Lacy about Noah.

"What did you whisper to him?" Beth asked.

"None of your business!" Lacy replied. "Nosy cow!" Lacy proceeded to get her compact mirror out of her handbag and also lip-gloss, she turned the top and brushed a smooth layer on her top lip and then repeated on her bottom lip, she looked in the mirror and her lips glistened pink in the light.

"He's only been turned a day, and you're already all over him!" Beth whispered.

"It's not like that!" Lacy shoved the mirror and lip-gloss back in her bag, and pushed it back under the table between her feet. "I've had to watch him admire Lucy for ages, and now she's out the picture I can finally make my move!"

"What does Roxy think of it all?" Lacy gestured to Beth to keep quiet, but it was no use Roxy had overheard that part and was instantly intrigued by the sound of her own name.

"What do I think about what?" she enquired, looking from Beth to Lucy, she got no reply at first. "Well come on, tell all, there's no secrets between friends!" Lacy remained silent. Beth decided to fill her in.

"Lacy has a crush on Noah!" Roxy looked slightly shocked. "Didn't you see them at break?"

"No, why what happened?" Roxy wanted more information on the matter. Beth began to tell her, when Lacy took over, but also added that she'd secretly liked him for a while now, about a year in fact. Roxy thought about it for a moment.

"Interesting...!" Roxy said at first. Lacy looked worried, without anything being official, Roxy was a kind of leader, and she didn't want to make her angry. "I suppose I prefer you to Lucy!" Roxy giggled. Lacy relaxed. Just then Mrs West entered the room.

"Sorry I'm late, but we have a new student joining our lessons." Walking behind Mrs West was a girl with longish black hair, and dressed in black from head to foot. This made her look mysterious, and like a Goth. Some of the other students laughed. There were Goths at the school, and they were all singled out and mocked by all the others, they were considered outsiders and freaks. At lunchtime they all sat on their own table, in the far corner. Nobody else sat at that because it was wobbly, and as no one would let the Gothic students sit with them, they had no choice. They'd got used to it, and had learned to completely ignore rude comments.

Roxy and her friends studied her carefully. They looked her up and down. Roxy sniggered as the new girl passed her, and she noticed a mark on her wrist. It was the same mark Roxy and the other witches had on their wrists. It looked like a scar, it was a W, with another W upside down over lapping it. The myth goes that the first witch to be identified by mortals in medieval times around 1542 was branded with this mark so people knew who she was and could avoid her. This practice lasted until 1712, when the last known witch was executed. Ever since then witches were born with this mark, and now acts as their sanctuary if they are ever lost or move to another town. They are able to show their identity and immortality to them without the use of spells, so mortals in the area didn't become suspicious. Roxy and the others kept theirs covered with sweatbands and bracelets.

"Hey you!" Roxy said. The girl turned and looked at her with a blank expression. "Come sit here!" addressing the seat behind her. The girl didn't speak; she stood for a moment just looking at Roxy. Roxy flashed her the mark on her wrist discretely, with that the girl sat where Roxy had suggested, as she did, Roxy turned to speak.

"So what's your name?" The girl didn't look up; she was rummaging around in her bag.

"Raven, my name is Raven," she replied. She glanced up briefly, straight into Roxy's eyes, and then continued looking in her bag; eventually she pulled out a pen.

"Great, well if you want you can join us at lunch!" Paige said. Roxy and Paige looked at each other, and mouthed the word weird to each other. Raven didn't reply. During the rest of the lesson she remained quiet, the others tried to speak to her, but she didn't really respond to them. The lesson ended and it was now lunchtime. Roxy and the others made their way to the canteen to meet the boys, Raven followed close behind them, Beth and Lacy kept turning around to look at her. She didn't see them, she was looking at the floor. Before they went in Roxy took her to one side, Lacy, Beth and Paige left them alone.

"Raven, have you ever been to school before?" Roxy asked. Raven looked at her, she hesitated, trying to avoid eye contact but finally answered her.

"No, how'd you know?"

"Just a guess…" Raven looked at her. Roxy thought she looked like a lost child, very naïve and vulnerable. "We don't really talk to mortals, we are also friends with werewolves, and my brother is one of them."

"I know I probably seem strange, but this is all new for me," Raven confessed.

"Not at all…" Roxy said. "Well a little, don't worry you can be friends with us, we'll help you settle in, and maybe take you shopping!" With that Raven laughed. Roxy did too, and she felt as though she'd prejudged her, and that she deserved the benefit of the doubt. They both entered the canteen; just behind them were Jack and Lucy.

"Look at him over there with them, they're not even his friends!" Jack said. "I'm going to go over and say something!" He was just about to storm over, but Lucy grabbed his arm and dragged him back.

"Jack, don't, there's something going on, and we've got to find out what!" she said. Roxy noticed they were staring over with cold looks of hatred.

"Who are they?" Raven asked Roxy.

"They were friends of my brothers," she replied pointing to Noah. "That's Noah, in Sanford if you're a witch or a werewolf you can only associate with witches and werewolves, mortals have to be cut out of your life, they can't know about us or vampires!" she explained.

"And what happens if you do?"

"You can be exiled, but if it's a werewolf, they can be sacrificed, in the past they used to exile the mortals too!" While Roxy was explaining this to Raven, she kept her eyes fixed on Noah and Lacy, who were sat together talking, and then they swapped mobile numbers. Lacy caught Roxy watching, and she looked worried, but Roxy smiled. She was looking forward to grilling Noah on this later at home. She also noticed Lucy watching them too, and she felt even better.

Raven remained with the young Sanford witches for the rest of the day. She tried to be careful in what she asked at first, she wanted to get their trust, and being invited to their cavern would be the first sign of trust. Roxy was hesitating in making that suggestion, she wanted to tell her mother, Anne, about Raven first, as it was Anne that decided who could join them in the cottage. It was known to them that there were witches who made alliances with vampires, or just generally had a bad agenda. Roxy and the other girls knew protecting their town was important to their parents, and also to them.

Before the next lesson started Roxy left the others and went into the girls' toilet, Lucy saw her get up and decided to follow her and confront her about what was going on. Roxy was stood over a sink concentrating in the mirror topping up her make-up; she was applying her usual pink lip-gloss when she noticed Lucy stood next to her in the corner of her eye. She put the top back on her lip-gloss, placed it back in her bag, turned and looked at Lucy with disgust.

"What'd you want?" she asked in a horrible tone. Lucy hesitated, but finally answered, she wanted to choose her words carefully.

"Why is Noah hanging around with you lot all of a sudden, and completely ignoring me and Jack?" She tried to copy Roxy's stance, leaning against the counter with her hand on her hip.

"None of your business, so get over it!" Roxy walked towards Lucy. She tried to pass her to get out of the door, but Lucy cut her off and stepped in front of her.

"That's not good enough, I want to know!" Lucy met eye contact with Roxy. "Now!"

"You told me to be a better sister so I am, I invited Noah to join us today, told him Joel and the others would welcome him, on one condition that he stopped hanging about with you two losers, and he jumped at the chance!" She smiled as she could see tears were beginning to fill Lucy's eyes. "The truth hurts doesn't it, now you know why I usually lie!"

"You're a cruel heartless bitch, I don't believe you!"

"Don't, I don't care really, just stay away from him!" Roxy made it to the door and opened it. She was just about to walk through when Lucy spoke again.

"You don't tell me what to do, and you can't control Noah, setting him up with Lacy isn't going to work, he loves me!" Roxy grinned to herself and then laughed. Lucy looked confused.

"I'm not controlling him, and I certainly didn't set him up with Lacy, that was a surprise for even me, but rather her than you!" With that Roxy left, as she did she could hear Lucy burst into tears, and she laughed even more. When she returned to the others she told them, she thought that Noah would show some weakness and affection towards Lucy, but he just shrugged and joked about it with Joel. Jack overheard the whole conversation and was shocked by Noah's reaction. He now felt hatred towards him, and had the urge to walk up to him and hit him, but he managed somehow to resist.

School came to an end rather quickly after lunch, and on the way home Roxy grilled Noah about what was happening between him and Lacy.

"So you and Lacy, already!" she glanced at him.

"What about me and Lacy?"

"Nothing, good choice!" She paused and then continued. "Apparently my sources tell me she's liked you for some time!"

"Really!" Noah replied, he sounded excited and surprised by this.

"Yep, who'd have thought, my little brother, the stud!" Noah told her to shut up and they drove the rest of the way in silence.

Seven

The next few days were more or less the same as Monday. He'd also discovered that he didn't turn into a werewolf every night. He did on Monday night, it was a strange feeling one he'd never felt before. They had come across some vampires, but Noah was advised to stand back and observe. Noah had also told Caleb about his English teacher, Mr Fisher, he too was concerned. So Noah and Tyler were given the responsibility of following him.

It was now Wednesday night, just coming dark. Noah was stood on the edge of the path at the bottom of the street where their school was. It had begun to rain, it was only drizzling at the moment, but Noah could tell by the big grey cloud that was heading towards the town that it would soon get a lot heavier. Winter was definitely on its way, there was an ice-cold breeze, and every time there was a gust, Noah's eyes started to water and his nose ran. He imagined that his nose resembled that to Rudolf, bright red. He looked at his watch, quarter past six. 'Tyler should be here by now,' he thought. It was their second night spying on Mr Fisher. The previous night they had stood outside his house and it had proved to be pointless; it was clear to them both that he must have gone somewhere else after leaving the school, before coming straight home. Tonight they were trying something different, waiting for him and following him to see where he went. Mr Fisher didn't drive so they thought best to follow him by foot. Another ten minutes passed, and then finally Tyler came into view coming around the corner. The rain was coming down a lot faster, and it was almost dark.

"So do we just wait here for him to come out?" Tyler asked, as he approached Noah.

"Don't think so because then he will see us…" Noah paused as he thought. "I've got an idea!" he said as he entered the school grounds, Tyler followed, wondering where he was going. Just as Noah and Tyler turned round the side of the building Lucy and Jack were walking past, they'd just been to the cinema to see a scary film that had just been released.

"Hey wasn't that Noah and Tyler going round the side of the school?" Jack said pointing.

"I don't care any more!" Lucy replied. Noah and Lacy were getting closer more and more every day, and she was pretending as if she didn't care, but Jack could tell that she did, no matter what she said. Jack talked her into following them to see what they were up to.

Noah and Tyler were now crouched under the window outside Mr Fisher's classroom. Noah peered in, to confirm that Mr Fisher was in there. He was fumbling around in his desk, Noah also noticed that he was shaking, and looked extremely agitated.

"How long does it take for a human to turn into a vampire?" Noah whispered.

"Dunno, exactly a few days maybe!" Noah looked back in the room and noticed he was now covered with sweat, and all of a sudden he swept everything off his desk and on to floor, in some fit of rage.

"I think tonight's the night for Fisher…look!" Noah suggested, with that Tyler joined him and peered in also.

"I'd say you're right, never really seen it before, but I have heard they have some kind of fit of rage and anger… a bit like we do!"

Just then Noah and Tyler heard a rustle in the bushes behind them, both of them turned around immediately.

"Did you hear that?" Noah asked.

"Of course I did idiot, I'm a…" Tyler cut off his sentence, he didn't want to say it, just in case it was someone that shouldn't hear it. Noah sniffed the air, unfortunately whoever it was, were downwind and he couldn't pick up a scent.

"Let's be careful, I mean won't they come for him when he's turned!" Noah whispered.

"Yes, they'll take him to their hide out, they won't have taken him yet, because we could have easily have got that out of him if we wanted. Vampires are very vulnerable, when they turn!" Tyler replied. Noah thought he'd said this a little too loudly considering they thought that someone was in the bushes listening in. They heard another rustle. Noah saw Fisher leave the classroom, as he shut the door Noah stood up. And turned his gaze to the bushes, he suddenly found himself fearless, and also curious. He walked slowly in direction of the bushes. Tyler joined him. When they reached it Noah hesitated for a moment before glancing round, he saw Jack and Lucy crouched behind it.

"What are you doing here?" he asked looking slightly furious.

"What are you two doing here more like?" Jack said as he and Lucy stood up.

"That's none of your business, now leave or you may regret it!" Tyler said, moving next to Noah.

"Is that right, where's your new girlfriend?" Lucy said addressing Noah. He didn't respond, both Noah and Tyler turned and walked away, they knew that Fisher would soon be leaving the school and they had to find out where he was going. They stood with their backs against the wall. Tyler looked round the corner, after a few minutes Fisher came into view.

"Who are you spying on?" Jack said they had continued to follow them, determined to get an answer.

"We have said that's nothing to do with you, but this is dangerous, you can't be here, please leave for your safety, go round the back though!" Noah said, Lucy could sense a glimmer of sincerity in his eyes; he kept his stare with hers for a moment.

"OK fine, come on Jack, let's leave the weirdoes to it!" They turned and walk round the back of school out of view, but they just went round the corner, Lucy felt this the right moment to find out what was going on.

"Who are they calling weirdoes? I ought to show them a thing or two, they haven't gone you know I can still smell them!" Tyler whispered.

"I know me too, we can only tell them so much though I guess. I will speak to Roxy about a memory potion, if they see or hear anything they shouldn't, no one else needs to know!"

"That's breaking the law in our world mate!" Tyler said.

"That's why we'll keep it between us, for our sake and theirs, although it's not our fault they followed us and won't leave!"

"Try telling that to elders!"

Tyler went back to watching Fisher. It seemed as if he was waiting for someone, and just then a figure appeared by a tree at the front of the school, Tyler was sure he was either in the tree, or landed next to it, he told Noah. Noah bent down on his knees and peered round the corner. The strange man and Fisher were talking. Noah and Tyler couldn't hear what they were saying, but given their body language it was important. They talked for some time, and then both of them looked in the direction of Noah and Tyler, they quickly moved back behind the wall. Noah's heart began to race, he closed his eyes and in his mind he was praying they didn't see them.

"You boys shouldn't be here!" The creepy voice echoed in Noah's ear, and it sent shivers down his spine, his heart started to race and he felt goose bumps all over his body. Noah opened his right eye slightly and saw a tall man stood over him, with long white hair, and glowing yellow eyes. He sniffed the air. "You boys are young werewolves aren't you?"

"What's it to you?" Tyler said. The man just grinned at him.

"Dorian!" Fisher bellowed from the front of the school.

"I'm here!" Dorian bellowed back. They could hear Fisher heading in their direction. He finally reached them and looked from Tyler to Noah.

"Are these boys students of yours John?" Fisher hesitated and finally he answered Dorian's question.

"Yes, Tyler and Noah!" Noah could tell Dorian was thinking. And at that point Noah thought that this was the end of him.

"I'm going to let you go…." He paused and then continued. "This once, but next time you won't be so lucky." With that Dorian and Fisher leapt up past the trees and vanished.

Tyler and Noah set off walking home. As they reached the bottom of the street Noah glanced up at the town's church clock, it was almost mid-night.

"Well that was pointless, we didn't find out anything!" Noah said, Tyler didn't reply. Noah heard a noise to his left and stopped, he put his arm out to stop Tyler too.

"What?" Tyler said. Noah was paying more attention to the man opening the door to the newsagents.

"Who's that, and why is he going into the shop at this time of night?"

"I don't know, maybe it's the owner!" Tyler replied.

"No it isn't, he's too tall!" Noah moved to left side of the road, slowly and quietly, he knelt down behind a car to watch, Tyler followed. When the man had entered the shop and shut the door, Noah and Tyler walked up to the window. Both Noah and Tyler looked through the glass. At first they couldn't see anything it was too dark, and then the man switched a light on. He had his back to them, and he was looking for something. Then another man appeared from the back.

"I can't find it Isaac!" said the younger man.

"Well you'd better look harder!" The man that spoke with authority and anger resembled that of Dorian, in fact the hair was the same and the eyes were the same colour.

"Vampire!" Noah whispered to himself. He was beginning to learn that certain vampires had a similar image, but others like Fisher and Noah presumed this man, didn't.

"They haven't been on the list for some time." The young man sounded nervous.

"Fisher was unlucky, this is the only chance we have left!"

"I know, I'm trying, there will be old records here somewhere, and he keeps them for at least two years!" The man looked as though he was shaking. As Noah listened in, the more he listened he began to realise he recognised the man's voice.

"No way, it can't be," Noah whispered.

"What, what is it?" Tyler asked.

"Well, that sounds like Joshua, he's the assistant to Mr Holland, the old guy who owns this place. I thought I hadn't seen him in here for a while!" The young man stood up and turned to side to speak to Isaac and it confirmed to Noah that it was Joshua – a nineteen-year-old who worked in newsagents. He'd always been nice to Noah, spoke to him and joked with him, whenever Noah went in the shop. He couldn't believe his eyes. He wondered why him, why did the vampires choose Joshua? Then he realised that when he and Roxy had followed their father, it was Joshua he'd seen chasing them. This made him more determined to find out what was going on.

Isaac was getting more and more agitated, which made Joshua nervous. He rummaged through some more files, eventually he stood up with a sheet of paper in his hand.

"I've found it!" he said, he couldn't help but smile, gloating at completing his task. Isaac turned to face him.

"Excellent, Drake will be most pleased!" He took the sheet from Joshua and looked at it. "This won't go without reward Joshua, especially after John failed, we must return and give him the address!" Both of them left out of the back, leaving the mess behind them, and the front entrance unlocked. It would look like burglary in the morning when Harry Holland came to open up, even though nothing was stolen. Noah and Tyler looked at each other for a moment, they were confused.

"Whose address do you think they stole?" Tyler asked.

"I don't know, but it sounded like it was very important!" They started walking back down the street again, trying to think between them who they could be after.

"Maybe the Mayor!" Tyler suggested, Noah didn't reply but gave him a look that was clear to Tyler he disagreed. They got to the street where Noah lived and they decided that they should tell Greg what they'd heard in the newsagents, and about the confrontation with Dorian.

They sat in the living room, Anne was in kitchen making tea for them all, and Roxy had also joined them. Neither of them interrupted Noah and Tyler while they explained in detail of the events of the evening. The only part they missed out was that Jack and Lucy were also there. Noah was anxious to speak with Roxy about her memory potion; whatever the vampires were planning he didn't want them caught up in it.

"What were the names of the vampires?" Greg asked.

"Dorian and Isaac," Noah replied. Greg couldn't hide the expression on his face that suggested he knew whom the boys were talking about. Roxy noticed it first.

"Do know them Dad?" she asked. Greg hesitated before answering his daughter.

"Yes I do, they caused a lot of trouble here some time ago, one hundred years to be exact. Back then they had a leader named Charles, he had a son..." Noah cut off his father.

"Drake, Isaac mentioned him earlier, by the sounds of it he's taken his father's place."

"Why, vampires can't die, can they!" Roxy said.

"They can, only werewolves can kill them!" When Greg spoke he smiled at Noah and Tyler. The sound of Anne dropping a mug on kitchen floor broke the moment's silence, she picked up the pieces and placed them in the bin, and proceeded to bring the tray of tea and biscuits into the living room, she placed it on table and turned to Greg.

"Don't, they don't need to know tonight Greg it's a long story, they know enough as it is!" Anne didn't want her children or the other young witches and werewolves involved in anything remotely dangerous, the other witch elders agreed. It was the only thing the elders disagreed on, Caleb, Greg and others thought it best they learned now and be a part of it, so when their time came to take over they would have the experience they needed to protect Sanford successfully. She turned to the teenagers sat on the sofa.

"Time for bed it's late and you've all got school in the morning, Tyler you'll stay with us tonight. I've told your mother, the fold out bed in Noah's room is already made for you!" They protested, but were overruled, Greg knew he could tell the boys at the den, Anne couldn't interfere there, and he knew the boys would tell the girls. He was proud of Noah, how he wanted to get involved and help, he could see the beginnings of a future leader in him, and ever since Noah was born that's what he'd always wanted for his only son, it was all Greg could think about. He knew that Roxy was the same and that she too one day could be a great leader for the witches, because of this he desperately wanted them to know the history of their community and above all his reasons for why he believed Drake had returned to Sanford.

Eight

Noah lay in his bed wide-awake, the sound he could hear was Tyler's snoring, and although he could stand the sound, because his mother and father both snored. It irritated him so much he couldn't sleep, whenever the occasion rose where he had to share a room with either of them, or on holiday when they were in a tent, but it wasn't the reason he was still awake. The evening's earlier events circled in his mind, the question that nagged at him and that he longed to answer was whose address they needed and why? It also annoyed him that once again his mother insisted on keeping things from him. He could sense that they both had an idea or even knew what the vampires were up to.

There was a tap on his door; he turned his head as Roxy entered. She looked at Tyler she pointed and giggled with Noah about his snoring.

"I need to ask a favour!" Noah whispered.

"Sure what?" she replied.

"Well, Jack and Lucy followed us, just on the school grounds, I think. I don't know if they saw Dorian, but I think to be safe you should do your memory spell or potion, whatever it is!"

"I suppose, but it is difficult to do, I might talk to them to find out first what they did see and hear!"

"No, I will, I'll get better luck, hopefully!" He lay back against his pillow, and looked up at the ceiling again.

"What do you think it was all about though?" Roxy asked. "Whose address were they after?"

"I don't know, but Mum and Dad do, I could tell!"

"Yeah I could too, Mum doesn't want us getting involved!"

"Dad does, he was annoyed when she demanded he shouldn't tell us." He thought for a moment. "That night we followed he wasn't mad like I thought he would be; he was glad, which also reminds me, the vampire that chased us!"

"What about him?"

"It was Joshua, I knew he looked familiar, at that the time I couldn't think where from, but after tonight I'm sure!"

"Oh my god, he's such a nice guy, sort of a family friend!" Roxy said, there was a hint of shock in her voice. "I better get back to bed, we will find out what's going on I promise you that!"

"You read my mind!" With that she left the room, and returned to her own. She could hear her mother and father whispering, her room was next to theirs, she put her ear up to the wall and tried to listen in, but it was no use, she couldn't hear what they were talking about. She got into bed and tried to fall asleep, but just like Noah there was too much going through her mind that she couldn't sleep. She worried whether she would be able to do the memory potion; it's tricky if you're not an experienced witch. She knew she would need help from her friends. She hoped that Lucy and Jack didn't hear or see anything. She tossed and turned, trying to get comfy. She had a thought, she sat up in bed, after a few minutes she got out and went to her door. She listened to make sure no one was up, then she opened it carefully, trying not to make too much noise, crept out slowly and then went downstairs. Without switching on any lights she went into the living room. She walked straight up to the book shelf and switched the lamp on that stood next to it. Then she carefully scanned through all of the books, on the third shelf down she found what she was looking for. Her mother's book on spells and potions. She sat down on the sofa, she looked at the contents page, to find what she wanted, and there it was, *'Potions and spells on memory loss: page 309.'* She flipped through to page 309, and read the page carefully; she eventually found the paragraph that gave her the information she needed.

It is possible to perform and spell, for long term memory loss. Although it isn't advised. There are ways in which the person in question can regain their memory, either through dreams, a certain word or image relating to the memory, can restore that memory. This spell isn't recommended to be used on mortals, as there is the danger of erasing their whole memory, they may forget who they are, where they live, and their friends and family. Hash consequences come with this, as it is a violation of mortal rights, (See page 189).

There are two ways to perform this, either by spell, or if preferred potion.

Potion list:-

1 Teaspoon of Phoenix tears (do not use any more than recommended)

2 Tablespoons of Maple sap

4 leaves of Snapdragon (White and yellow

A Myositis bulb

2 cuttings from a Flame Nettle

Roxy sighed as she read the ingredients list as she knew they wouldn't be easy to get hold of, most of them were rare. She put the book on the coffee table folding the corner of the page with the potion. She walked over to the desk in the corner at the opposite side of the room and rummaged in the drawer until she found a map. The map noted important witch and werewolf locations, including towns and villages that only inhabited witches and therefore had shops where she could get the ingredients. The town that was closest to Sanford was Witch Haven. She knew her mother went there regularly for rare things used in potions and spells. She thought for a moment. She took the map and the book upstairs with her; she switched on her bedside lamp. She reached for her phone and sent text messages of her plan to her friends. She left out Raven, if they got caught she didn't want her getting into trouble for missing school when she'd only just started, she let her know though, so she didn't think she was leaving her out.

The plan was for Noah to give their teachers sick notes, stating that they had all got food poisoning after going to a Café after school, their parents would think that they had gone to school as normal. But they were going to go to Witch Haven to get the ingredients they needed. She had decided that she didn't want to take any chances, if they left it too long, it would give Lucy and Jack time to tell people what they saw and heard. And that would mean Tyler and Noah would be tried before the elders, and they wouldn't go easy on them, even though it wasn't really their fault. She received messages back, they were all in on the plan, and Raven understood why she couldn't go. This gave her chance to talk to Noah, and find out more about him.

At the Castle Raven proceeded to let Giselle know what her school friends were up to.

"Well I want you to follow them, I want to know what potion they making!"

"But Roxy is right I can't really miss school…" She was cut off.

"Why do you care? You didn't want to go in the first place!" Raven didn't answer, she didn't know why she cared, and she just did. "Right, well that's final then!" With that she left the room, not long after Sebastian entered, to find Raven slummed in a chair deep in thought.

"I know why you care!" he said smiling.

"What?" Raven replied. "I don't care, I have a job to do, and that's to figure out what they're up to, and what they know." Sebastian walked to the other side of the room near the fireplace, huge flames came from it, and the heat was immense but Sebastian couldn't feel it.

"You're lying, you care because they have accepted you as part of their group, and now you finally know what it's like to be a teenager, going to school being around people your own age, and what's more they're witches, just like you!"

"How'd you know that?" she asked.

"I've been around long enough to know what humans long for, even witches."

"Were you ever human?"

"Me human no, I was a monster. I didn't have a heart, and didn't respect the life of other people, that's why my fate was to become a vampire after death."

"How'd you die?"

Sebastian turned away from her; he wasn't so sure he should be telling a young teenager these things. But then he thought why not, she asked and she's nearly grown up.

"I was burned, that was what happened to murderers in those days, I still don't regret it though."

"You're right you were a monster, and doomed to be one forever after death, I guess that's why you're now a vampire, still a murderer!"

"No, now it's survival, I need the blood of humans to live, would you call a lion a murderer if it attacked and killed a human for feeding?" She didn't reply. "I guess not!"

"So is that the case for you all then, except the ones you've turned yourselves?" Raven stood up, she'd never really spoken to any of vampires, and so she took this chance to ask the questions she'd always wanted to ask, to try to work out for herself if this was the right side to be on.

"Yes, except Drake of course, he was born a vampire!"

"How was that possible?" She moved a little closer to him, but not too close, she knew if she asked a question he didn't like that he could lash out, and it would be fatal.

"His mother was bitten by a vampire, while she carried him you see, and when he was born, she started to show signs of the turning. His father killed her, but he couldn't kill the baby, he took the baby to the forest and left him there. The vampire that bit his mother had a connection with him, and he took him in, his name was Charles. He named the baby boy Drake, and brought him up to be his heir if necessary!"

"That's horrible, leaving a baby in the woods alone!"

"Oh don't worry, Drake took his revenge, at that tender age, his human father was his first kill, and it's more terrible what he did to him!"

"How'd you mean!" Sebastian paused, looked at Raven and knew that he definitely shouldn't tell exactly what happened to Drake's father.

"Let's just say, he's still suffering in the dungeon!" Sebastian was just about to leave the room, when he turned and spoke again.

"You can't trust your new friends, as soon as they find out who you live with, they will hate you just as much as they hate me, and with that you too will become their enemy!" Sebastian left the room. Raven knew what he had said was true, and somewhere inside she didn't want that to happen. She liked having friends her own age, she also knew if she betrayed the vampires they would show no mercy, and she'd end up in the dungeon. She didn't know who was in there, or what the vampires did to them, but every other night she was being kept awake by screams of agony. She shuddered at the thought and then returned to bed.

Nine

The morning seemed to take forever to arrive, and Roxy was already awake when her alarm went off. She immediately switched it off, and went to Noah's room. She knocked on the door and then opened the door. Noah was sat on his bed.

"I sent Jack and Lucy messages last night, they won't tell me whether they heard or saw anything strange," he said as soon as Roxy shut the door.

"I need you two to do a favour for me!" she said without acknowledging what Noah had just told her.

"Sure what?" he replied and Tyler nodded in agreement.

"Well, last night I was researching the ingredients for the memory potion, and some of them are really rare, I need to go to a town called Witch Haven to get them." She paused to see what they thought so far, when she got no response she continued. "The girls and I are skipping school, we've written a sick note from our parents, will you two hand them in for us?"

"Yeah sure!" Tyler and Noah both said.

"Noah if you could tell them I feel really bad and that I was up all night…"

"You look like you were!" Noah suggested, she nodded to let him know that she was. She handed Noah her note, and then went back to her room to get ready for her trip. She went straight to her wardrobe; she began to rummage through the junk that lined the bottom, until she found what she was looking for. She pulled out a tattered old shoe box, she took off the lid, in it was her passport, her birth certificate and the paper counterpart of her driving licence. Underneath her important documents was an envelope, she took it out and placed the box back in her wardrobe. Inside the envelope was a big wad of money, around it was a rubber band.

She had got the money cleaning the house of an old lady that lived across the road, on Tuesdays and Thursdays after school, and if she found herself with nothing to do on Saturdays and Sundays. Her name was Thelma, at first Roxy didn't want the job, but her Mother persuaded her. No one else knew about it, she didn't want people to know how nice she could be, especially since she'd started to enjoy it. She'd got know Thelma well over the past six months, and enjoyed her company, and her stories of World War II and what young people used to do in those days. In a way it made Roxy realise how lucky her generation is to have things that are now available to them, and not take it for granted, as she found it hard to imagine not having mobile phones, computers and the many other gadgets she couldn't live without, including most of all her hair straighteners. Thelma was well into her eighties; she refused to go to home as she could look after herself. Just the everyday cleaning she used to be able to complete in a breeze, had now become a daunting and almost impossible task. She had terrible arthritis in her legs, and Roxy had started to notice that was now sleeping downstairs. She had suggested on a few occasions that she should get a stair lift installed, but it was no use, Thelma was stubborn. Roxy also knew that she was strong minded and she wanted to try to carry on being as independent as she could. She liked that about her.

With the rubber band still binding the money she put it in her purse. On the floor was a pile of clean clothes, she shifted through the pile and found her favourite pair of skinny jeans. She pulled them on, and then picked out a short-sleeved top, and put a shirt on over it, but didn't button it up. She picked her Ugg boots up and sat on her bed while she pulled them on. She got her keys and bag then left her room and went downstairs. Noah and Tyler were already eating breakfast. Joel was giving them a lift to school, but Roxy drove them to the end of the road so her mother didn't suspect anything. She proceeded to go pick up Lacy, Paige and Beth. Lacy was waiting outside for her, when she got in the car she was anxious to find out how Noah was. Roxy told her what had happened the night before.

"So whose address were they after?" Lacy asked.

"We don't know, they never said!"

"And Josh, I thought he was a nice guy!" Roxy didn't say anything. As she turned down Paige and Beth's road, they could see them strolling down the pavement towards them. Roxy stopped and they got in.

"Isn't Raven coming with us?" Beth asked as Roxy turned down the road out of Sanford.

"No, I don't trust her yet!" The other girls all looked at her with surprise.

"But you're the one who made friends with her!" Paige said.

"I know, but we have to be careful, vampires never work alone!" No one said any more, if Roxy didn't trust anyone neither did anyone else. Lacy had the map in her lap; she was trying to follow it carefully as there were no signposts for Witch Haven. It was about an hour long drive to the small secret town in the middle of the countryside. They had been driving for half an hour when it began to rain.

"Oh great I didn't bring an umbrella!" Paige said, crossing her arms in a sulk. Beth glanced at her, and giggled to herself.

"Why don't you trust Raven?" Lacy asked.

"I don't know!" Roxy replied trying to concentrate on the road ahead.

"You don't distrust someone for no reason!"

"What, Roxy you don't trust Raven, then why is she friends with us?" Paige added.

"Look I don't know, just a feeling, I'm trying to find that out myself!" As Roxy spoke her mobile rang.

"Lacy grab my phone out of bag, I got a message!" Lacy reached on the floor for Roxy's bag, and rummaged round for her phone, when she found she read the message.

"It's Noah; he wants to know if Raven is with us!"

"Why I thought Roxy told her to stay at school!" Beth said, sitting up to read the message over Lacy's shoulder.

"I did, see sometimes you've got to go with your instincts," she replied.

"Something might have happened!" Lacy said. "I'll call her!" Lacy got her phone and scrolled down her contacts list until she got to Raven's number. Missy had bought Raven a mobile when she discovered that she would have gone to school. The phone rang but there was no answer. Little did they know Raven was flying above them on a broomstick directly above the car, so as not to be seen. Raven felt guilty and somehow it didn't seem right to be following the girls she classed as her friends. As the week had gone on she often thought about telling them the truth. But she was torn, she knew if she did either Giselle or Drake would find out. She couldn't bring herself to imagine what they would do. And Sebastian had made it clear that if Roxy and the others found out, their friendship would be over.

"She's not answering!" Lacy said. Her voice suggested she was concerned

"That's not a good sign!" Beth said.

"Maybe she's just upset that we didn't invite her!" Lacy said. They turned down a narrow road. Roxy could tell that there was a small town up ahead.

"I think this is it, and when we get back I think it's time I had that awkward talk with Raven!" The other girls all knew what that meant. Roxy had a way of telling if people were lying or not. And they knew Roxy wasn't nice to people who lied to her. Roxy found a parking place on what looked like the main street. There wasn't much space, but her car was the only one in the street, and in the town from what Roxy could tell. They got out of the car and looked around, there were only two people in the street and both just stood and stared at them. One of them was a frail old woman; she needed a walking stick to steady herself. Roxy could tell instantly she was a witch, she had the traditional look, with a black cape. It looked tattered even from a distance – her hair was long and looked as though it hadn't been washed in some time. The other woman was a lot younger; she was wearing ordinary clothes.

"Yep we are in the right place!" Paige said. Roxy lifted her arm to reveal to both women they were witches, both nodded and carried on about their business. They walked up the street towards a small shop on a corner. There were herbs and bottles in the window. The bottles contained thick liquids, of all different colours. One was red, another blue, and the third was a dark liquid that looked like it was from a river or lake. The sign above the door was very faded and it was hard to make out the letters. They came to the conclusion that it read: 'MISS RIDDLE'S RARE SUBSTANCE STORE.'

"She didn't put much thought into the name!" Lacy said, peering in through the filthy window.

"At least we know we've got the right shop!" Beth added. "If that is what it says!" They opened the door, as they did, the bell above rang. When they were all inside, an old woman appeared from round the back. She was old and haggard, when she finally reached the counter, she could barely see over it.

"What you want?" she said.

"Are you Miss Riddle?" Paige asked. The woman didn't answer straight away, she looked at the girls in a concerned way.

"Maybe, why you ask?" she finally said.

"We want these items!" As Roxy spoke she handed the woman the list of ingredients, she tried to sound as polite as she could, but for Roxy that didn't come easy, she also made sure to show her mark on her wrist.

"Oh, yes dear I'm Miss Riddle!" She picked her glasses up off the counter, and placed on her nose. She read down the list.

"Sorry about the rudeness, some people have been using this stuff wrong, and blaming me when it goes wrong, thought you were the witch police." She looked at the girls again. "You're not are you?"

"No, we're still at school, my mum sent us to get these for her!" Roxy said.

"Well I do have some of these, but there's another shop round the corner, that's where you will have to get your Phoenix tears, and Maple sap!" She came round from behind the counter and walked up to a shelf. There were a number of boxes on every shelf, each labelled. Riddle took a box off the second shelf up; she took it to the counter and opened it. She got a small plastic bag from her left side of the counter, and placed four leaves from the box in the bag, and then she handed it to Roxy.

"That's your Snapdragon, it works better crushed, but it depends on what you're using it for!" Roxy shrugged to give the impression she didn't know what it was going to be used for. Although she got the idea that Riddle won't care what it was being used for, just that she was making a sale, by the look of things she hadn't sold much in a while. Miss Riddle went back to the shelf, and took two small boxes off the shelf this time; she took them back to the counter, and repeated what she had done with the Snapdragon.

"There's your Myositis bulb, best if you cut it in small pieces, and finally your Flame Nettle, most potions tell you to heat it to get the liquid out, be careful not to overheat it!" Roxy took the bags. She paid Riddle with a twenty-pound note. Riddle took it without saying anything, and then gave change. The girls thanked her and turned to leave.

"Be very cautious when using memory potions, don't use it if it's not necessary. Especially when mortals are concerned, hash consequences come with it!" she said. Roxy turned and the look on her face suggested to Riddle that she was right. "I maybe old, but I'm not stupid, just mind yourselves girls, make sure you know exactly what you're doing, I'd hate to hear that something terrible had happened!" Roxy smiled and nodded, Miss Riddle smiled back, and then went into the back again.

"She was creepy!" Lacy said.

"She was nice!" Roxy said. The others looked at her in disagreement. "She knew what we wanted this stuff for, she could have refused to sell it to us, and we are teenagers after all!"

"Fair point!" Paige said. "Hope the next shop assistant isn't a creepy, weird old lady!"

"Do we really need to go through all this trouble, we don't know for certain Jack and Lucy even heard anything!" Beth said.

"I know, but I'm not taking any chances, and if they continue to stick their noses into everything I want to be ready, plus I don't trust Raven, there's enough to use on ten people. I'll use some on her if it comes to it!" Roxy replied.

Unknown to Roxy and the others, Raven was behind them, creeping slowly into the shop that they had just left.

"Miss Riddle!" she said as she entered the shop.

"Raven is that you?" Riddle's voice came from the back, and then suddenly she appeared. "How are you dear?"

"Good thanks, were there four girls in here before, about my age?" Raven asked.

"You always get right to the point, you must have picked that up from Crystal!"

"Miss Riddle please!" Riddle could tell Raven was already getting inpatient.

"Yes, they just left!" Riddle kept eye contact with Raven.

"What were they here for?" Riddle didn't answer, she just kept looking at Raven, the more she looked the more worried and frightened she seemed to get. "WHAT WERE THEY HERE FOR?" Raven shouted. Miss Riddle seemed startled at the outburst.

"I think it best you leave!" She backed away from the counter and slowly went into the back.

"Sorry, I just need to know what they wanted that's all!" Raven was beginning to get more and more agitated.

"Where do you live now, or more to the point who do you live with!" There was fear in Riddle's eyes.

"Giselle and the others... like I always have!" Raven knew what Riddle meant, and she knew without a doubt Riddle knew that she shared a castle with vampires. Miss Riddle had the power to read minds.

"You lie, I know, now get out!"

"Look I just want to know what they were here for, then I'll go!" Raven calmed her voice, and spoke as though it was a desperate plea, as though she was begging for food.

"I won't tell you anything, you traitor!" Riddle went back to her knitting in the back.

"Fine, you old hag!" When Raven left she slammed the door. The slam of the door got the attention of Beth, who immediately turned around.

"Oh my god, it's Raven!"

"Where?" Roxy said in disbelief. As she glanced behind her, she saw her. Roxy said nothing and stormed up to her.

"Hey, what you doing here?" Roxy asked.

Raven hesitated at first. "My Auntie is sick, we used to live here and she trusts Miss Riddle's remedies, only she doesn't do it any more!" she replied.

"Really, oh that's a shame!" The tone of Roxy's was slightly sarcastic. Just then Miss Riddle appeared at the entrance to her shop.

"You'll do well not to associate with her!" Riddle said to Roxy, then she gave Raven a cold look of hatred. Roxy noticed this, and for some reason, she believed the old woman. She had been suspicious of Raven ever since she met her. Riddle looked back at Roxy. "Those feelings you keep having, go with it, it's more than just instinct!"

"What do you mean?" Roxy asked, but Riddle had already gone back into her shop. Raven looked at Roxy and grinned.

"Riddle is the village nut around here!" The other girls had joined them.

"She seemed alright to me!" Roxy said. Raven didn't look at her, but Roxy kept her eyes on Raven. "What was she talking about?" Raven looked as though she had no idea what Roxy was talking about. "When she said that we'd do best not to associate with you?"

"I told you she's crazy!" She looked at the floor, she could feel her heart pounding her chest, and the palms of her hands were beginning to feel clammy. "She doesn't know what she's talking about... Just ignore her!" Roxy thought for a moment, and decided that the phrase keep your friends close and your enemies closer applied in this situation. She ordered Raven to stay outside the shop while they went and got the rest of the substances they required for the potion.

Walking back to the car Raven thought she would try getting the information she needed straight from the horse's mouth.

"So what's all this stuff for?"

"Things our mums need, they didn't tell us what for!" Paige quickly replied. Raven nodded.

"If you tell me what you got I may be able to tell you what it's for!"

"No that's OK; we don't poke our noses into what our mums do!" Beth said.

"Aren't you curious?" Neither of them responded. They all got into the car, and drove back to Sanford barely talking. Roxy kept staring into her rear-view mirror at Raven.

Later that night Roxy told Noah what had happened in Witch Haven, he didn't have much to say on the matter. But he agreed with the concern Roxy had about Raven, and suggested they keep a close eye on her.

Meanwhile at the castle Drake was growing angry with the witches, especially Raven.

"Drake is disappointed in you, you've got close to them, but you don't know what they're up to, and you still have no idea which of the werewolves could be the one we are after!" Giselle's voice was full of rage and anger.

"They aren't stupid, they don't trust me yet!" Raven said, her voice was quiet and shaky with fear.

"Well make them!" Giselle shouted, as tears began to fill Raven's eyes. "You know what will happen if you don't, and believe me, we won't go down with you!"

"It's not that easy, especially since Riddle saw me there, she knows, and she warned them about me!" Raven saw the fury in Giselle's eyes. She walked over to shelf and took a vase, and threw it with force to the floor, it shattered into pieces. Raven jumped in her seat.

"You useless incompetent child, I knew you couldn't do it!" Just then, Crystal opened the door and stormed in.

"Giselle that's enough, she is just a child, and don't forget you made the suggestion to Drake. It won't be Raven that will pay, it'll be you!" There was a moment of silence. "Or is that what you're so worried about?" Giselle remained silent. "Raven come on time for bed!"

As Raven and Crystal left the room, Raven thanked Crystal.

"Don't mention it sweetie!" They walked up the stairs, and Crystal promised she'd help her.

"How?" Raven asked.

"I don't know yet, I'll figure something out, and a way for us to get away from here, it's not right you being here. Missy also agrees, don't know if she'll join us, but she'll help!" Raven smiled and went to her room.

Ten

Noah was getting ready for school. He looked outside it was still dark. Winter had arrived. As he got dressed his mind begun to wander. His parents were still refusing to include them in their plans, only the werewolf elders were allowed to go the den, the girls weren't allowed to the cavern either, and he thought sooner or later the humans would notice the vampires, as there were more of them than ever. He felt frustrated, as though despite what the elders told them, they should be doing something help. They just kept saying it was too dangerous, and he didn't understand why. During the night he'd had another dream. It was Josh, Fisher and Drake. They were lingering outside a house. He knew he recognised it, but he couldn't think whom it belonged to. They were talking about the people inside and how they were going to get in. Vampires can't enter a home unless they are invited. He didn't think it too important, but it reminded him he still hadn't spoken to Caleb about his dreams, he hadn't had the chance.

"Come on, we'll be late!" Roxy burst in full of energy. He didn't reply just nodded.

"What's with you lately?"

"Nothing, just feel as though we could be doing something to help… don't you?" He put on his shoes and walked over to the door.

"What can we do exactly? We don't what's going on!"

"We could try and find out, why aren't any of the others interested?" He turned to look at Roxy who was still stood in his room.

"Because this is what it's like, they solve the problems and get rid of it, then when things are fine again, they teach us!"

"Teach what? With you I can understand, but us werewolves could learn better by fighting!" He huffed in anger and went down the stairs. He went in the living room and sat down. Roxy followed.

"I know what you're saying, but it is dangerous, if you don't how to fight a vampire they can kill you easily!" She waited for him to speak, but he remained quiet. Anne noticed they hadn't come for breakfast. She went to living room.

"Aren't you two having breakfast?" Roxy stood up to and went to the kitchen. "Noah!"

"I'm not hungry!" he said, he kept his stare at the floor.

"You have to eat something, get your strength up!"

"For what? Sitting at home and doing nothing? You won't even let me go see Lacy!"

"We've been through this, it's too…"

"Dangerous, I know, but how else are we supposed to learn, get experience?" Anne didn't speak; she turned to join the rest of her family in the kitchen. Noah sat by himself until it was time to go to school.

He got into Roxy's car. He was feeling frustrated and angry. He tried to hold it in, so as not to take on the people he cared about but he was finding it hard. Roxy had tried to create small talk, but it was no use, she got no reply from Noah but grunts. When they arrived at school, Lucy was stood a couple of feet from the car. He tried to avoid looking at her, but he couldn't resist. She looked back, he gave her a half smile, but she turned away. He remembered the night he'd kissed her, and didn't blame her for still being angry at him, turned away and went and sat by the tree with his friends. He kept glancing back towards Lucy and Jack as he met Lucy. He got the feeling that they were now in a relationship, their body language was more than friendly, and he strained to hear what they were saying to each other. The surrounding noise of other students shouting and laughing made it difficult, so that he heard nothing.

"What's wrong mate?" Tyler asked, speaking quietly so no one else could hear him.

"Nothing, just feel as though there's something we could be doing."

"Don't worry about it, it's not our problem!"

"What!" Noah shouted. "That's the thing it is our problem too!" Everyone that was in the area all looked round at him, including Lucy and Jack.

"Don't say it too loud will you!" Joel said. Noah could sense hostility in his voice, normally Noah would back down, but he found himself getting more enraged.

"Why, everyone will know soon anyway, they are starting to take over!" Raven didn't say a word, but she was slightly nervous, she thought the same as Noah. But she still couldn't decide which side she was on. Noah stormed off on his own, Lacy wanted to follow him, but she stayed with rest of the group. He went into the school and into a classroom, as he walked to the window he kicked a chair. He heard the door open; he turned his head to see Lucy standing in the doorway.

"What was that all about?" she asked moving closer to him. He ignored her, and continued to stare out of the window. "Noah, talk to me... does it have anything to do with the night last week?" She waited for answer, she knew he would talk to her.

"You don't know anything about that!" He paused. "You've got no idea!"

"Well then tell me!"

"I can't, I'm sorry!" He looked at her as he spoke.

"Why? I don't understand!"

"You're not supposed to!"

"What's going on, tell me why you're suddenly best friends with people who used to make your life miserable?"

"I can't!" he shouted. As he did Jack appeared from round the corner, he went to Lucy and put his arm around her, tears had begun to fill her eyes.

"Come Lucy, just leave the prick alone!" She turned into Jack's chest, and pressed her face against him as tears rolled down her cheeks.

"You two seem to be getting close!" Noah said, but it wasn't friendly.

"Well I didn't kiss her and then the next day wake up as someone else!"

"That's not what happened, Jack!"

"Well it seems that way to me, unless you want to put me right that's how it will always be in my mind!" He and Lucy turned to walk away.

"I can't!" Noah's voice had calmed, and was shaky as he was sad, Jack turned to glance at him. "I want to, but I can't!"

"You used to tell us everything!" Jack replied.

"I know, and I hate having to keep this from you, and not be able hang round with you both like before, but this is how it has to be, it wasn't my decision!"

"You can, we won't tell anyone!"

"They'd know, and it's not worth it, what will happen to me and to you if I do!"

"Who are they?"

"It doesn't matter, I think it's best if you go now!"

"What have you got yourself into mate? Sounds like you need to get out of it!"

"Nothing, look I've already said too much!"

"Alright, if you need to talk or need any help, just ask and I'm there!"

"Thanks, just be careful and watch your backs, especially at night!"

"Will do mate!" Jack smiled at Noah, and he smiled back. After they had left Noah felt alone, and slightly isolated. The school day went by like any other, except Noah spent it alone. At lunch Lacy had tried to talk to him, but it was no use. In the car on the way home, he didn't say a word to Roxy. He'd thought that she would have agreed with him earlier at school, and would want to find out what was going on just like he did. But she was content with sitting back until their parents decided to tell them, she'd tried to convince Noah that they eventually would, but he didn't believe her. When they got home Noah went straight to his room and stayed there, he didn't even go down to dinner. He was lying on his bed nearly drifting off to sleep when his mobile phone rang; he sat up and pulled it out of his pocket only to find that it was a reminder. Tonight was the night he, Jack and Lucy went the cinema. They went the same night every month. He clicked it off and put it back in his pocket. He put his hand up to face and rubbed his eyes, sighed and then walked over to the window, he pulled back the curtain. As he looked out he noticed a shadow under a tree across the street, at first he thought nothing of it. Then he thought about Lucy and Jack walking alone at night, and vampires that would be looking for their next prey. There was no way he could just sit here in his room assuming they would be all right and make it home. He put on his shoes and grabbed his jacket, he ran down the stairs to front door.

"Where are you going?" Anne asked. She had emerged from the kitchen as she'd seen him walk past.

"Nowhere, just for a walk!" He opened the door, and shut it behind him as he left. He'd got to bottom of the drive when he heard his father's voice.

"Noah, get back inside, don't be stupid!" Noah stopped, he thought about going back, then thought to tell Greg where he was going and why, but he found himself walking down without saying a thing. It wasn't far to the cinema, and he'd set off in time to see Lucy and Jack arrive safely and go in, they were holding hands. Noah thought he might be jealous, but discovered that he was happy for them both. He then thought about Lacy, and how he'd upset her. He got out his phone and began to send Lacy a text message apologising to her, and adding they should go out somewhere at the weekend. She took a while before she answered him; she agreed that it would be nice to spend time alone. He smiled to himself, and sat down by the tree; he looked up at the stars, and took deep breath of fresh air. As he sat he noticed that the streets were unusually quiet, apart from Lucy and Jack, he'd only seen three other people. The third was the man stood across the road, he was leaning against the wall next to entrance to the cinema, and Noah watched him. He didn't know how, but he knew he was a vampire, possibly waiting for the people to leave, or maybe someone that was alone, who had just gone to corner shop for some milk so they could have their usual morning coffee. It wasn't long before the man noticed Noah. He stared at Noah. It occurred to him that he possibly seemed like the perfect prey, a teenage boy sat alone in the dark, but Noah didn't move, he remained where he was, and suddenly found himself staring back. Did this man know too? He thought that Noah was a werewolf, that he was inexperienced. And then he wondered if vampires ever drank the blood of werewolves, he shuddered at the thought and decided to get up, walk away, and come back when the film had finished. He walked in the opposite direction to the vampire. He didn't get more than two feet when he heard footsteps behind him, the vampire was following him, stalking him, and he knew this was it, he would have to fight even though he wasn't sure how to kill a vampire, or how the vampire could kill him. He knew it had happened before, even though it was rare for a vampire to kill a werewolf, it was always the young inexperienced werewolves that were unlucky.

He began to run and quickly turned a corner, as he did he felt a burning sensation sweep over his body and before he knew it, he had turned fully into werewolf. It was the first time he'd turned fully and he liked the feeling. He sniffed the air around him, he could smell the vampire approaching, and he stood up straight and faced him as he came round the corner. The vampire stopped for a moment, and then ran at full speed towards him. Noah did the same. He slashed the vampire with claws, and found that he healed almost instantly. Unknown to him vampires had sharp long fingernails that were used in the same way. The vampire dug them into Noah's side, he howled and eased off with pain, the vampire took this opportunity to grab Noah. He held him tight as he pushed off the ground and took Noah 100 feet into the air; the vampire hovered for a moment.

"Let this be a lesson boy, don't fight a vampire unless you know what you're doing!" The vampire let go of Noah. "But you're not going to live long enough to learn that lesson!" Noah fell fast through the air, he began to regret disobeying his parents. Then suddenly he found himself slowing down, he realised that he was gliding. It was strange for him, he didn't recall ever being told that he could do that. He finally reached the ground and landed safely much to the vampire's surprise. Noah looked at him as he knelt on all fours where he had landed, and he knew now what he had to do, this was what he'd dreamt about before he turned. He bounded towards the vampire and jumped on his back. The vampire fought back, slashing Noah more and more. He fell of his back, but Noah didn't give into the pain like he had before, this time it made him more enraged. He stood up and struck the vampire in the head with full force. The impact of the blow had broken the vampire's neck, and in doing so had split his spinal cord in two. It seemed that was enough to kill a vampire, he lay motionless on the ground. Noah turned back into a human again. He walked up to where the vampire lay, and nudged him with his foot, there was no movement, and moments later the vampire's body turned to dust and blew away on the breeze. Just then Logan appeared.

"Noah, are you alright!" Noah felt immense pain in his side, he touched his wounds and there was blood on his hands.

"Yeah I think so, better than the vampire anyway!" When Logan reached him he put Noah's arm over his shoulder and they began to walk down the street.

"Your parents are worried sick about you. That was a stupid thing to do!"

"I didn't know we could do that, glide through the air!"

"We can't, but it appears you can!" They turned round the corner and continued past the cinema, the film had finished and people were leaving to go home including Lucy and Jack.

"How come it's just me that can do that?"

"I haven't the foggiest, but tonight you should be thankful that you can, because otherwise you'd be dead!"

"That's how they kill us isn't it?"

"Yep, but they'll have to come up with a new trick to kill you!" Logan laughed. As he did Lucy and Jack came running towards them.

"Oh my god mate what happened?" Jack said in shock.

Noah thought for a moment about his answer.

"I was attacked by a group of thugs!"

"Why, you weren't stupid enough to provoke them were you?" Lucy asked.

"Nope just a classic case of being in the wrong place at the wrong time!"

"He'll be fine, why don't you two get yourselves home, as quick as you can and be careful!"

Noah and Logan finally turned down Noah's street.

"Will I be OK?" Noah asked.

"Oh yeah, good as new in the morning, promise, you're in for a rough night though!" Logan noticed the confusion on Noah's face.

"Vampires heel quickly, for us it takes a bit longer than that and it's painful!"

"Can't wait!" Noah laughed, and then stopped himself when it hurt too much.

"You seem in a good mood, for someone who's just been attacked by a vampire!"

"To tell you truth I am, I wanted to prove that I'm strong enough to fight!"

"Well you've certainly proved that. I don't think your parents will agree straight away, but I will do my best to convince them that you did really well, despite the injuries. In case I don't get a chance to tell you later, you were very brave, and fought him with skill, which is strange, and both remarkable!"

"When I landed I knew I would beat him, I had a dream a while ago, it didn't make sense then, but I realised that it was that fight!"

"Your dad told me about your dreams, that's also just you, did you already know you glide then?"

"No, my dream started with me knelt on the floor!" Logan looked at Noah, as they reached the drive.

"You're special, different from the rest of us, and I'm proud of how you fought tonight, I'm sure Caleb will be too!" They walked up to the front door, Logan opened it, and called out as he entered.

"I found him!" Logan shouted as he entered the house. He took Noah to living room where Greg and Anne were sitting, relieved that their son was now home. Roxy came running down the stairs. Noah went to lie on the sofa.

"What happened?" Anne said, rising to her feet.

"He took on a vampire!" Logan answered standing in the entrance, Roxy pushed past him to see what had happened.

"Are you stupid you could have been killed?" Anne said, looking now at her son, who was clutching his side. Logan moved towards Noah in his defence.

"He's alright, the vampire isn't though!" Logan glanced over at Greg who was smiling with pride.

"It would seem Noah can fly, well glide anyway!"

"What how, why?" Roxy said in shock.

"Don't know, but it saved his life!" Anne looked confused, she didn't seem to take in the words, or couldn't believe what she was hearing.

"Thanks Logan, for killing the vampire!" Greg said he moved over to his friend to hug as a gesture of gratitude.

"No worries, but I didn't kill him, Noah did!"

Greg turned instantly to Noah. "That's my boy, well done!"

"Greg!" Anne said, she didn't think that it was appropriate to congratulate Noah for what he had done.

"Anne no werewolf has ever killed a vampire without training and observing others, or glide to the ground safely for that matter!" Logan nodded in agreement with Greg.

"He told me he knew how because of a dream he'd had!" Logan added.

"I knew my boy was special, and different!" Greg couldn't hold in his excitement.

"I best be going, see you tomorrow!" Logan said, and then he left. Anne paced the room.

"Roxy, help Noah to bed, he's in for a rough night!" Greg ordered. Roxy nodded and helped Noah up off the sofa and then up the stairs. As they reached the top they heard Anne telling Greg he was still going to school, and then Greg assure her that he'll be fine in the morning. Noah got into bed; he fell asleep as soon as his head hit the pillow. Roxy went to her room and texted all the others what had happened.

Noah found it hard to relax and get comfortable; he tried to focus his attention on something else. But it was no use. After a few hours it began to ease, and he drifted into a deep sleep.

At the castle Drake was getting anxious, he'd sent Tom and Ethan into Sanford to go hunting and neither had returned. Dorian entered the room where Drake was sitting.

"You better have news on Tom and Ethan, or else I don't want to know!" He didn't look at Dorian, he continued to gaze out of the window, and he looked weak. With the werewolves patrolling the town at night, they hadn't had fresh blood in a while.

"No, not yet!" Dorian had waited a few moments before he'd answered, he knew Drake wouldn't like it. Drake slammed his fist on the table next to him. He didn't reply, but he looked furious. There was a knock on the door, Drake gave permission for Sebastian to enter the room, close behind was Ethan.

"Ethan has returned my Lord!" Sebastian said.

"Excellent, where's Tom?" Drake answered.

"He's dead, I saw it!" Ethan said, he kept his gaze at the floor.

"Who killed him?" Dorian asked, looking at Ethan, hoping he would acknowledge his presence. It took a few moments for Ethan to register what Dorian had asked.

"I don't know. I didn't recognise him!" He thought for a moment. "He was young, a teenager, and he...!" Ethan couldn't complete the sentence, he was still I shock.

"He what?" Dorian moved closer to Ethan, he put his hand on his shoulder.

"He flew, well glided to the ground and then finished Tom off, I didn't know they could do that!"

"They can't!" Drake said he was now looking at the three men. "But one can, just one!" As he spoke the second time he turned back to the window. Sebastian looked at the clock, one more hour and the sun will be starting to rise.

"We should get to our coffins, soon it will be sunrise." He walked over to the door, Ethan and Dorian followed. "Aren't you coming Drake?"

"Not just yet, I need another moment or so, the boy will soon know, and so will they, he already knows he can glide!" He sighed, things weren't going quite to plan. "How's Josh and John getting on?"

"Great, they have the idea of visiting the other towns near here!"

"Give it more time, another night or so!" Sebastian nodded, and left the room. He walked down the corridor, at the other end was a black door, Sebastian opened it, and descended down the stone staircase. In the cellar there were five rooms, two for the leaders, three were for the hunters, and Drake had one to himself. Sebastian entered the room second to the left, Carlos was just getting into his coffin.

"Sleep well my friend!" he said, as he began to close the lid.

"You too!" Sebastian replied.

Drake just made it to his coffin in time; he quickly climbed in and closed the lid. The sun began to rise over Sanford, bringing a new day, no one waking up knew what had happened the night before, and best that they didn't.

Eleven

He was in a dark room, the only light was that of the moon. It shone bright enough that he could tell he was in some sort of dungeon. And as he looked round he could see the walls were damp, and patches of mould covered most of them. There was a big oak door to the right of him. There was a smell, one he did not recognise, he guessed it was the damp. He felt strange and found himself bringing his hand up to his neck, he could feel two puncture marks. When he brought his hand down and looked there was blood on his fingers. He slowly started to move towards the door, first he pressed his ear against it. He heard nothing, then he tried to open it, but it was no use, it was locked. After a few moments he heard footsteps, he pushed his ear against the door for a second time. The footsteps got louder, and then they stopped outside the door. He took a few steps back, and waited as a key turned in the lock. Slowly the door began to open; he took a few more steps back, until he reached the wall behind him. In front of him stood a tall figure, and he froze, not being able to take his eyes away from the stranger stood in the doorway. Eventually the stranger stepped forward right into light of the moon, Noah gasped, he knew who he was, Drake. This time his eyes looked brighter, and his large pointed fangs were visible.

"You have been brought here," he said with a pause, as if trying to exact as much fear as possible from his victim. "Because you may have information useful to me." Noah was confused, and shook his head.

"Don't play games boy, you have two choices, tell me what you know, or … Well I think you can guess the alternative," Drake said in the coldest voice that Noah had ever heard, so much so, shivers ran up and down his spine. "All I really want to know is where he lives!" Noah shook his head again, still confused.

"I… I don't know who you're talking about!" Noah's voice was shaky, but it was then he realised that the voice wasn't his own.

"I know you know, you used to be friends, if I'm not mistaken!" Drake stepped closer, he was now breathing in his face. The smell of his breath made Noah wrench, and he very nearly threw up. When he finally composed himself he realised that Drake's breath had a strong, stale metallic odour, that of blood. Noah found himself mumbling but not being able to tell what he was saying. Drake seemed satisfied with what he said and left the room, slamming the door shut as he did, and he heard the lock click. It was then Noah woke up. His body was dripping with sweat as usual, and he felt cold. He tried to piece together the dream, but it was no use, the pain from his injuries earlier that night was growing stronger and stronger, he lay back on his bed, and looked at the clock, 4 a.m. This time he wasn't afraid of the dream like he had been before, he had a feeling they meant something. The fight he'd the night before with the vampire proved it. This time instead of trying to keep awake, he tried to fall asleep again. When he shut his eyes he tried to get Drake back in his mind, and also the dungeon, but it was no use, the harder he tired the more awake he felt. He sat up and reached for the glass of water Roxy had left for him and took a sip, returning the glass back on his bedside table, he leaned back against his headboard. Who was it in the dream? he thought, it wasn't me. And he also wondered who Drake was after. He couldn't really think clearly with the pain. So he just sat there in the dark, staring at the wall opposite, until he could feel his eyes become heavy again.

He stirred as the sun rose, he heard Roxy in the bathroom getting ready for school, and Greg opened the door.

"Hey how are you feeling?"

"OK, I think," Noah slurred half asleep.

"I managed to talk your mum into letting you stay at home today!" Noah didn't respond, with that Greg left the room, and went downstairs. It was nearly lunch when Noah woke again; he knew his mother would have gone to meet the other witches by now, so he went downstairs. He went straight the kitchen, rummaged through cupboards and the fridge but there was nothing he really wanted, and when he thought about it he wasn't really hungry. There was a knock that startled Noah for a moment, he walked into the hallway and picked the keys up off the table, and before he unlocked it he decided to ask who it was first. "Who is it?" he waited for a reply.

"It's Caleb!" With that Noah opened the door.

"My dad isn't here!"

"I know. I came to see you!" Caleb replied. Noah let him in and they both made their way to the living room, Caleb took seat with Noah across from him.

"How are you feeling?" Caleb asked.

"OK I think, still hurts but it could've been worst!"

"Logan told me about it, about everything!" Noah didn't reply. "He said you knew you would beat him, that you saw it in a dream!"

"Yeah, that's right!" Noah paused, he could tell Caleb was waiting to hear more. He told him about the dreams, when they started, he told him about the dream he'd had in English and the one the night before.

"That's interesting, do you know why?"

"No, when I found out I was a werewolf I thought that could be the reason, that all werewolves had dreams like that, until my dad and Logan both told me that's not right!"

"No we don't Noah, you're special very special, with the dreams, which I think are actually visions, and the gliding, none of us glide either I'm sure Logan told you that too!" Noah nodded. "I think I have the answer, there's a legend that says if a werewolf is bitten by a vampire, he will become ill very ill, but it won't kill him, the venom from the bite will run through his blood and become part of his own!" Noah listened intently as Caleb continued. "It won't affect him, but it will affect his future bloodline, and they could have a telepathic link to the vampires, and also adopt their ability to fly. These werewolves will the strongest of our kind and vampires won't stand a chance against them, the only way a vampire can kill one of us is by dropping us from a great height!" Noah knew what he was getting at.

"So if a werewolf can glide there's no way they could do that!"

"Exactly, your father Greg was bitten by a vampire, way before you or Roxy were ever born, and I think that's what's happened to you!" Caleb saw Noah's face light up, as he was told he couldn't be killed by a vampire. "The visions, the ability to glide, things have changed over the years though. Witches have teamed up with vampires, and they are probably trying to find another way. There is something else that can harm us, silver. Drake can probably sense you too, as you'll have a link with him – he's their leader. And so he will not want you to be a threat to his plans!"

"So, you want to stop him before he finds out about the silver?"

"Yes, any information you can give me about his plans would be great Noah!"

"I don't know yet, it's like that bit keeps being missed out of every vision I have!"

"I understand, they should become stronger, like the one you had last night, you said you could smell things and that's never happened before!"

"If anything about the plan comes clear, you'll be the first know, but I want to help, I want to be a part of our plan to stop him!"

"I understand and by having these visions you are!"

"I mean I want to fight!" When Caleb didn't speak Noah continued. "I want to protect people, my friends, there's no way I want any of them to come face to face with Drake, like in my dream!"

"You are very brave Noah, and I'd love for you fight with us, but it's not up to me, you're not eighteen yet and until then it's up your parents whether you can or not!" Caleb looked into Noah's eyes and saw a bravery and courage like none he'd seen before. Noah was a warrior by heart and he knew this. Noah reminded him of a young Caleb, who also wanted to fight the vampires desperately.

"I will speak with them, see if I can bring them round, anyway it's not father who needs convincing, he's told me many times that he longs for you to join us properly." Caleb stood up. "Well I'd best leave you to your rest, I will be back later when your mother returns, and I will try and make her see the bigger picture." Noah smiled.

"Thanks!" Caleb smiled back and nodded. After Noah had locked the door again, he went back to bed, and fell back asleep.

Twelve

Roxy was stood by the oak tree, she was alone, and watching the entrance to the school like a hawk. She was waiting for Raven to leave. She had plans to either confront her or follow her, and at this point she wasn't sure. She was shaking from the adrenaline, all the thoughts that had been going through her mind over the past few days, were now about ready to burst out of her. Lacy and the others had tried to talk her out of it, that Raven was nice and could be trusted, but Roxy wouldn't listen. She had a gut feeling that told her they were wrong. She began to pace. 'What's taking her so long?' she thought. Just then Raven came out of the double doors of the school and began to descend the stairs. Roxy was so enraged by the sight of her that without thinking she found herself striding towards her.

"Raven!" she shouted in her most angry, unfriendly tone. Raven was stunned by this – the reaction that Roxy was looking for – to catch her off guard. "I want to know why you were in Witch Haven the other day." Roxy was now stood right in front of her. Raven could smell her peppermint breath from the chewing gum she had just spat out.

"I… I told you why I was there!" Raven's voice was shaky and she avoided any eye contact with Roxy.

"I don't believe you!" Roxy was studying Raven's face for the telltale signs of lying. She could already tell she was from the no eye contact and the shaky voice, she wanted to know how much was a lie. She focused on Raven's forehead for signs of perspiration, and in which direction Raven's gaze was. If it was left then it meant she was searching for untrue images, a lie. To the right would mean she was searching her memory, which would indicate she was telling the truth. Raven kept her gaze straight down towards the ground, looking neither left nor right. Roxy's anger grew more and more.

"You better start telling me the truth, because believe me I will find out!" Roxy shouted. Raven stepped back and thought for a moment what Giselle had taught her.

"Don't threaten me, you have no idea what I'm capable of!" Raven glared into Roxy's eyes.

"Oh I think I do, you know dark magic, and most the witches in Witch Haven do!"

"What are you talking about?" Raven said trying to look as though she was confused.

"I went back there, you used to live there with three other witches, what I want to know is why you are here!"

"It's none of your business!"

"That's where you're wrong, this is my town, and we're good people here, protecting people, from the likes of you!" Raven shook her head at Roxy, turned and walked away. Raven knew now where she belonged and it wasn't with Roxy and her friends, even if deep down that's where she wanted to be.

"Not for long!" Raven said as she turned the corner. Roxy set off to go follow her. When she turned the corner Raven was nowhere in sight. It was a street with no other corners; she walked down the street towards the bend. 'She must have gone down there.' She thought, 'there's nowhere else she could have gone.' She started down the dirt track, which had huge trees at each side. As she walked she looked ahead to where it led, and then she saw it through the trees, her mouth fell open with shock.

"No it can't be!" she said to herself. Through a gap in the trees she saw a tall castle, from a distance it looked derelict, but that didn't mean it was. She turned and ran back up the dirt track as fast as she could, she had to tell her parents what she'd discovered. As she ran back into town she looked over her shoulder to make sure no one had seen her, as she passed the school she slowed down, to catch her breath.

Thirteen

Roxy burst through the door. Rushing into the kitchen, and then into the living room. Her parents weren't at home, she went back into the hallway and towards the door.

"What's with all the noise, and rushing around?" Noah stood at the top of the stairs, wearing his pyjama bottoms and an old T-shirt. He was rubbing the sleep from his eyes.

"Thank god someone's home!" Roxy said with relief.

"Why, what's happened?" Noah asked, slowly descending the stairs. They both went into the kitchen. Noah sat at the table, while Roxy made them both a cup of tea.

"So where's Mum and Dad?" Roxy asked.

"Gone to a meeting with Caleb!"

"Why?"

"He came round earlier to talk with me, and said he'd speak to Mum and Dad about me joining the fight properly!" He told Roxy all about his conversation with Caleb.

"Wow, that's great news, at least you have an answer now!"

"Yeah," Noah replied with a smile on his face. "So tell me why you came home bursting through the door and dying to see Mum and Dad!"

"Well you know I have always had a bad feeling about Raven." Noah nodded. "After school I waited for her, and we had a confrontation, she didn't really tell me what I wanted to know!" she paused.

"That's to be expected Rox!"

"I know, I told that this was my town and we are trying to protect people, and she said not for long!"

"What do you think that means?" as Noah spoke he shifted in his chair.

"I have no clue, so I followed her round the corner but she wasn't there. It was that street to the left of the school, and I realised that there was only one way she could have gone, down that old dirt track that leads out of town."

"And then what!" Noah butted in.

"I didn't see her until I got a glimpse of that run down castle through the trees, she was greeted at the door by three very strange odd looking old witches, well actually one them looked in her thirties!"

"What are they doing in there, they can't live there surely not!" Noah said sounding surprised and excited at the same time.

"I don't know!" The room fell silent as they thought about what to do. Suddenly Roxy started to stand up, she looked stunned, and then confused.

"Maybe we should go have a look around there tonight, and find out!" As he spoke he looked out the window, and so didn't notice the expression on Roxy's face.

"That wouldn't be a good idea!"

"Why not, we need to know!"

"The… the vampires are in there!"

"Well that settles it then Raven can't live there… Hey how'd you know that?"

"Uh, oh Mum told me, when she was telling me about what happened the last time they were here."

"What's wrong Rox?" he said as he finally turned around and saw the disturbed expression on Roxy's face.

"You don't understand, Raven does live there, with those witches and the vampires, she's on their side."

"Oh my god, so she's been pretending to be our friend, to find out what we know, or our weakness or something!" Noah said in an angry tone.

"Yes, maybe all of them, and possibly also to find out if a werewolf like you actually exist here!"

"Well she doesn't know anything does she?" He'd begun to calm down.

"We need to hatch a plan to find out what they're up to!"

"How you've scared her away!" Noah began to pace the room, Roxy mirrored him.

"Maybe not, she knows I have a feeling, she doesn't know I followed her!" She paused to think, she stopped pacing and faced Noah.

"She won't trust us now though, and I certainly don't trust her!" Just as he spoke Greg and Anne had arrived home, and had opened the door to kitchen.

"Good news son, you're joining us big boys!" Greg stopped to get a reaction from Noah, when he didn't get one he became worried. "Noah did you hear me?" Noah snapped out of his zombie like gaze.

"What, oh yeah that's fantastic!" He walked over to his father to give him a hug.

"What's going on?" Greg asked, switching his stare from Noah to Roxy. Greg and Anne both sat down while Roxy told what she'd seen. Greg stood up and walked towards the kitchen door.

"Noah get dressed we need to tell the others about this!" There was hint of excitement in his voice that Anne picked up on. She knew exactly what her husband was thinking.

"Greg it won't be that easy, they have witches there for a reason." She paused hoping she wouldn't have to explain, but her family looked at her puzzled. "Witches can put protective spells around a building, the vampires won't want werewolves just waltzing in during their daily sleep, and they will still be activated at night, not to mention that you don't know how many vampires are in there. It's a castle!"

"You're right but we still have to tell them what we know!" Greg thought for a moment. "Is there a counter spell for these protective ones?"

"I can find out, I will get straight on it tomorrow!" Anne replied. "Roxy, you and your friends want to help us?" She turned smiling at her only daughter.

"What! Really?"

"Yes, if Noah and the boys get to join the fight, I don't see why you and girls can't too, after all this will be your responsibility after we're all gone, and we need everyone to pitch in if we're going to beat them and protect our town!"

"I'm definitely in; I will tell Lacy and the others!"

"It won't be easy!" Anne said as Roxy started texting on her phone.

"Yeah I get that, seems to be your motto lately." Both of them smiled at each other. In the meantime Noah had gone to get dressed.

"Come on Noah we've got to get going!" Greg shouted up the stairs. Noah rushed out of his room and down the stairs, and followed Greg out the door.

"Hey Noah guess what!" Roxy shouted in excitement. "We girls are joining the fight too!"

"Great, one big team!" Noah turned and walked round the passenger side of Greg's car, and jumped in. Greg backed the car out of the drive and set off down the road. Noah felt good about the information they had, and that he and Roxy were now included.

Fourteen

The rain was coming down fast. Noah had taken shelter under a tree. With protective spells surrounding the castle, there was nothing they could do. The werewolves were waiting for the witches to find a counter spell, and also locate the gemstone. Both were proving to be quite difficult. Christmas was a few days away, and they all knew what that meant, work parties, family parties. Lots of humans making themselves easy prey for the vampires. So Noah and the others were all on street watch, even Caleb was out checking Hillcrest Street. Noah was quite bored, nothing had happened so far and it was reaching 1 a.m. He was standing across from the cinema again, the same place he was when he met the vampire he'd killed. There were a few people on the street all making their way home, but so far he hadn't picked up any scent of the vampires. Finally he saw a figure walking towards him. He sniffed the air around him but it wasn't the familiar smell of vampires, it was Lucy. She had seen him too.

"Hi!" she said in the friendliest tone she could muster.

"Hey!" Noah replied. He watched as she walked past him without a glance. He took a deep breath and found the courage to talk to her.

"Lucy wait, can I talk to you for a minute?" She stopped and without turning to face him gave the reply.

"I have nothing to say to you!" She continued walking but only took a few steps. She stopped and then turned around. "Alright I'm listening!"

"I'm sorry about what's happened, I still care about you though, that hasn't changed!"

"Why did you kiss me that night?" she asked.

"Because… I like you, I always have!"

"But you knew then what was going on, it would have been better if you hadn't!"

"Why?"

"Because I like you too!"

"Really!" He sounded a little surprised.

"Yes, but what's the point, we can't be together, can we!" She turned back around and began to walk away.

"Let me walk you home, it's not safe this time of night!" He ran to catch up with her. They walked in silence. He kept glancing at her and she kept glancing at him.

"We could if you really wanted, you just couldn't tell anyone, not even Jack!" he suggested.

"Why, are you afraid that your new friends would not approve or make fun of you?"

"No, believe me it wouldn't be them I'd be worried about!"

"What do mean?"

"Doesn't matter, in fact you don't want to know!"

"Then my answer is no, if you're with someone you shouldn't have secrets, or worry about what people will think!" They had reached her house and she walked up the path towards the door.

"It's not like that!" he shouted after her. "You don't understand!" She turned her head.

"That's the thing I never will because you won't tell me!" She walked to the door and went into her house. Just then someone came from behind a tree. They were still in the shadows and Noah couldn't tell who it was.

"Why don't you leave her alone?" It took a few minutes for Noah to recognise the voice.

"Jack, is that you?" He walked closer to the shadows. "What are you doing here?" Jack stepped into the light. His eyes were strange, a pale yellow colour, Noah had never noticed that before, and then a horrifying thought occurred to him.

"Jack are you ... A vampire?" Noah's voice was serious and sincere.

"What, are you mad?" Jack laughed. "Vampires don't exist!" Noah looked at him more closely and smelt his odour. He reeked of Lynx and Hugo Boss. Which mixed together wasn't a pleasant smell, especially for a werewolf. And his eyes were now the dark brown they normally were.

"Of course not, I was joking, prowling in the dark, lurking behind trees, not normal behaviour you have to admit!"

"True, I was making sure Lucy got home OK!" Jack said with a grin on his face.

"Why, this town is safe enough isn't it!" Noah challenged, there was something about Jack that wasn't quite right. His mannerisms had changed slightly.

"Yep, but you never know do you!" with that Jack walked away past Noah and turned the corner at the end of the street. Noah followed him. Jack was walking further away from his house. Noah was hiding behind a tree and watched as he turned a corner. He was just about to follow him when a hand fell on his shoulder.

"What you up to?" It was Alex, and Callum was behind him.

"Following Jack!" Without turning to look at either of them he ran towards the corner and looked round before entering the street. Alex and Callum were at his heels.

"Why?" Callum asked. Noah explained how Jack's eyes changed from pale yellow back to dark brown, and his strange prisoner.

"Doesn't mean anything, you could have imagined his eyes changing, and if it was a vampire or turning into one you'd have smelled it on him, which you said you couldn't!" Alex explained. Noah thought for a moment.

"Do you where my dad, Logan and Caleb are?"

"Yeah, they are lurking outside the Kings Arms pub!" Alex replied.

"Great, thanks!" Noah said. He set off in the direction of the Kings Arms. When he reached the pub he scanned the area for them.

"Caleb!" he said. He repeated his name as they gave no reply. As he walked towards the entrance to the pub he saw all three of them in an alley.

"Noah, what brings you to this part of town?" Logan asked.

"I need to ask you something!" He paused as he was waiting for a response.

"Go head, ask away!" Caleb replied.

"You know when my dad got bitten by a vampire, and the effect it had on me, could the same thing happen if a human got bitten by a vampire and conceived a child before they fully turned?"

"Not sure, that's certainly never happened before!" Logan replied.

"It's possible!" Caleb suggested. "I think it's quite clear anything is, but why do you ask?" Noah told them about his meeting earlier with Jack.

"That's certainly strange, and you are sure his eyes changed like that?" Greg asked.

"Yes, very sure!" Noah looked at Caleb who was clearly deep in thought. When he noticed Noah looking at him, he stepped closer to him.

"You were very specific about how you think it's possible, care to enlighten me!"

"Of course, Jack doesn't know much about his father. Jack has never met him, his mum had told him, that a few days before she found out she was pregnant he had disappeared, no one knew where he'd gone or why, which was strange because he was very popular, and..." Noah paused.

"What?" Logan asked.

"Jack's father's name is Isaac. When Tyler and I had seen the vampire in the shop with Josh I knew he looked familiar, Jack is the spitting image of him."

"No that can't be possible surly not," Greg said with a stunned look on his face.

"It would seem it is!" Caleb said. "And if Isaac discovers he has a son he'll want to complete Jack's transformation!"

"You mean he isn't a vampire!" Noah asked.

"No not completely, just like you he'll have some of their abilities!" Caleb went into deep thought once again and an idea came to him. "I would like to meet Jack though, find out what he can do, he may be of use to us, being friends with you. Could you arrange that?"

"Yeah, I think so!" Noah reached into his pocket for his phone.

"Not now Noah he'll be asleep won't he?" Logan said having seen Noah's actions.

"I don't think so, I was following him around town, just a moment ago!"

"He'll be looking to fill the empty void, don't tell him about Isaac!" Caleb ordered. Noah nodded in agreement and sent a message to Jack telling him to meet him at the Kings Arms.

Fifteen

Caleb was talking with Jack in private, no one else was allowed in the den, but Noah was outside the entrance pacing. He wasn't sure if it was anticipation of their conversation, or the fact that he might have one of his best friends back. But he did wonder if that meant Jack wouldn't be able to speak to Lucy either. He shook the thought off, and decided to worry about that if it came to it. Drops of rain began to fall, they got heavier and heavier until it was throwing it down. Within minutes Noah was soaked, but he didn't care. It was not long before Caleb emerged out of the den with Jack at his heels.

"Jack is to join you on a night, I will be having a meeting with the other young boys, and Jack is to be treated as one of us and with respect!" Caleb said as soon as he saw Noah.

"What about Lucy?" Noah asked, almost immediately after Caleb had spoken.

"He can still associate with her, he's half vampire, and they have no laws or rules like that." Caleb paused. "Jack has, however, taken an oath that if he does mention any of this to Lucy or any other human, he will be severely punished, he has also sworn loyalty to us, being half human he still has compassion for them and wants to stop them."

"When this is over, for my loyalty, he's going to ask the witches if there's a cure!" Jack added, sounding excited.

"Is that what you want?" Noah asked and Jack nodded. "Because I like being different!" Noah added.

"Yeah but you're a werewolf, I'm half of a night prowling monster that feeds on humans!" Noah understood what Jack was saying, and he wouldn't like the thought of it either. "I just want to help you guys save the town and then get back to a normal existence!" The three of them walked back through the woods. Noah was sharing with Jack all that had happened so far, even his heroic moment, and also the turning of their teacher Mr Fisher and Josh.

"So that's why you and Tyler were hanging round the school that night!"

"Yep!"

"Look I apologise if I said anything offensive, I was mad at how you'd just ditched me and Lucy, now I realise it wasn't your fault and it was for a good reason!" Jack said.

"It's fine mate!" Caleb smiled at the boy's reunion. Just then Dorian appeared. Caleb jumped in front of Noah and Jack out of instinct and habit.

"Well well well, having a lovely stroll in the moonlight are we?" Dorian hissed.

"Boys, I want you to run, this is my fight, sorry Noah!" Caleb began his transformation from his human to werewolf form. Noah and Jack did as they were asked and ran; behind them they hear the howl of Caleb.

"Will he be OK?" Jack asked.

"Yeah, he'll be fine!" They kept running until they got to edge of the woods, they then stopped to catch their breath. They walked along the road that lead back into town. They got half way when they were stopped in their tracks. Josh had leapt out from behind a corner.

"Look what we have here!" he said. "The human and his lap dog!"

"I wouldn't call him that if I were you!" Jack snapped back.

"Why what are you gonna do, human!" Noah could feel the rage building up inside him, his blood boiled. And then he began the change. His hair grew longer and coursed all over his body, his fingernails also grew. His legs bent backwards like the hind legs of a dog. And last of all his ears pricked up and he had fangs. Instantly he howled.

"Wow!" Jack whispered. Josh sprang into action and jumped on Noah's back. Jack then fought Josh to try to get him off. Josh flung his sharp nails in Jack's direction, and made three deep gashes on Jack's right cheek. Noah's anger grew and he threw Josh off his back and caught him deep in his abdomen. He lay on his back on the road. Having known he'd won the battle Noah began to change back again. Both Josh and Noah watched in amazement as Jack's injuries healed before their eyes. Josh then scrambled to his feet, clutching his wound with his right hand he fled.

"At least you heal like they do!" Noah said, as they continued back into town.

"I can do everything they can do, except set on fire in sunlight, thankfully though I don't have their thirst for blood, therefore no desire to attack a human!"

"That's good then!" Noah replied.

"You were awesome mate, what's it like?"

"What the change… a strange sensation comes over you, along with rage!"

"Do you know who you are though, I mean in films they don't do they!"

"Yeah, that's why we don't attack people, because we live amongst them!"

"Cool!" They walked the rest of the way in silence and without any more confrontation. When Noah got home, he briefly thought about telling Roxy about Jack, but instead exhaustion took over and he went straight to bed.

Sixteen

When Noah arrived at school, he noticed Jack stood under the tree waving him over. Noah walked over to him.

"Hey mate!" Jack said. They started to walk towards school. "Did you tell your dad what happened last night?"

"Yeah, he said great work from us both, but given the situation we should have killed him!"

"What do you mean?" Jack asked.

"Well more and more people are going missing, they've either fallen victim to them, or they've become vampires!"

"Which is the most likely scenario?"

"Both, and both are bad, we don't need them getting their numbers up just as much as we don't need them preying on humans!" Noah replied.

"How are the witches getting on?"

"They are making progress, which is great considering they are looking for the location of the gemstone, trying to find a counter spell for the castle, and they have said that they will try and find a cure for you. They do think there is one somewhere!"

"Great, tell them I appreciate it!" As they entered the school Noah saw Roxy, Lacy, Beth and Paige stood by the lockers.

"Tell them yourself they are over there!" Jack walked towards them, Noah followed close behind.

"Hey girls, thanks for agreeing to find a cure for me!" There was a degree of shyness in his tone.

"It's OK, we're just glad you don't want be one of them!" Roxy said, she smiled as she spoke.

"I certainly don't after what I've seen and heard!" He paused with his thoughts. "It's horrible what they do, things that until recently I thought only existed in films!" Roxy put her arm around Jack as they walked.

"Welcome to our world Jack, a living nightmare at times, but if you read our stories and legends, you'll find we always win!" she said.

"At least there's a good ending to all this!" he said relieved. Just then Lucy burst into the corridor.

"JACK, JACK!" Lucy bellowed, as she stormed towards them.

"Hey Lucy!" Jack said.

"Why didn't you meet by the tree like you normally do, and why are you with them?" It was clear to Jack that she was angry.

"He can talk to whoever he wants, you're not his mother!" Roxy snapped.

"You!" Lucy said directly at Roxy. "Why are you stealing my friends from me, do really hate me that much?"

"Well Noah is my brother, blood is thicker than water, and Jack can do what he wants!" Roxy and the others turned to walk away.

"Why Roxy, tell me why you hate so much!" Roxy turned to her.

"Somewhere deep inside you know!"

"Is it because Noah likes me?"

"No, dig deeper than that, and let me know when you find it!" Noah said goodbye to Jack and went to meet Tyler. Noah's first lesson was History. He slowly made his way to the classroom, which was on the second floor of the school. He felt tired and as he entered 32A he made his way to the back and sat at the desk in the right corner of the room. As usual he started to doze off, but before he had chance to fall asleep Jack sat next to him.

"Guess what?" he said in an excited tone.

"What," Noah mumbled.

"Raven is back at school, Roxy just saw her!" The news woke Noah immediately.

"What, you're kidding!"

"Nope, just seen her approach Roxy in the hall!"

"That wasn't smart of her!" Lucy wasn't sat too far away, and moved to the table in front of Noah's as she'd been eavesdropping.

"Who's Raven?" she asked.

"Doesn't matter," Jack answered. He turned straight back at Noah. "What do think she's going to say?"

"I don't know!" Noah said. The lesson began and Mr Wright continued where he'd ended the last lesson, about World War II.

Roxy had almost exploded when she saw Raven back at school; she walked into the girls' toilet hoping Raven would follow. She hurried into the first cubicle but didn't shut the door and she waited. She could see the door from the reflection in the mirror across from her. It wasn't long until Raven followed, as she entered she called out to Roxy.

"Roxy don't be mad at me, I have something to tell you. I can help you and the others!" As she got closer, Roxy jumped out and grabbed him by the throat, and slammed her against the wall.

"I don't want to hear it, I've seen enough!" Roxy replied.

"I know you know I live at the castle, but I'm not there by choice, I live there with three other witches, Giselle, and her daughters Crystal and Missy!"

"So, why do I care?"

"They are nothing to me, I'm an orphan. I never wanted to live in that castle!"

"So then why did you say those things outside school the other night?"

"What? I don't know what you're talking about!"

"Don't treat me like an idiot, we spoke, you said some rubbish about how this will soon be your town and then I followed you to the castle!"

"I'm not lying, I have been ill for two weeks. I found out last night that Giselle had been pretending to be me!"

"How does she look like you, I swear don't push it, I could strangle you right now!"

"She knows a spell that will turn her into anyone she wants, so long as she has some blood. I don't really know what it is, but I've seen her do it before." Raven paused, when Roxy remained silent she continued. "Anyway while I have been ill, I got up sometimes in the night, I heard the vampires talking, and I know whose address they were after!"

"Go on!" Roxy said.

"You have to trust me!"

"I will trust you if you're right!"

"Well it's actually two addresses, a Jack Thorn, and Lucille Gomez!"

"Oh my god!" Roxy said under her breath.

"Do you know them?" Raven asked.

"My brother does, this better not be a joke, or trap, coz if it is…" Raven cut her off.

"It's not I swear, I didn't know who they were, I just didn't want anyone to get hurt!" Roxy turned and looked straight into Raven's eyes. She didn't get the vibe she got from before. She had a little trust in her this time.

"Come with me!" Roxy said as she ran out of toilets and down the corridor, Raven close behind her. They headed straight towards the double doors. A teacher tried to stop them.

"Where are we going?" Raven asked. Roxy didn't reply. They ran outside towards Roxy's car. She unlocked the car as she ran with a button on her keys, and jumped in the driver's side. She ordered Raven to join her. Raven got in the passenger's side. Roxy started the engine and drove out of the car park and turned left towards her house.

"We're going to my house you are going to tell my mum what you told me. If you're lying she will know!"

"Great, will she know what to do?"

"Yep, along with the other elders, I should warn you if you are lying or this is some sort of trap, tell me now, because they will know what your intentions are, Miranda is very good at that!"

"I'm not I've told you!" Roxy wasn't sure at this point whether to believe Raven or not. But Anne had told her that Miranda could spot enemies and lairs, even when they seemed truly sincere. They walked into Roxy's house and just like she had suspected her mother and the others were all sat in the kitchen.

"What are you doing you should be at school," Anne said as soon as Roxy and Raven entered the kitchen.

"Sorry Mum, but Raven has some inside information she'd like to share with you all!"

"Well go ahead do tell!" Miranda said as she stood up and approached Raven. "My daughter has told me plenty about you!" Raven told Anne and the others what she knew, and they all listened intently. When she had finished Miranda stood up again.

"Give me your hands!" she said to Raven.

"What?"

"Just do it, like I said if you're telling the truth you've nothing to be worried about!" Roxy explained.

"OK, sure!" Raven did as Miranda had asked. When she did something strange happened, something that Roxy hadn't seen before. A green mist surrounded Raven and for a moment Roxy couldn't even see her. Miranda turned and looked at Roxy.

"Your friend is telling the truth!"

"What would happen if she wasn't?" Roxy asked.

"The mist would have been red, and she'd have passed out!" Rachel cut in.

"OK first things first, what's Raven going to do now?" Angie asked. "She can't go back to the castle, the vampires will know she's betrayed them!" Anne thought for a moment.

"She can stay here with us, she will be safe here!"

"What about her clothes and things?" Roxy asked.

"I think her life and safety are more important don't you!" Angie suggested.

"I kind of knew that I wouldn't ever be able to go back, the protective spell alone wouldn't let back in, so this morning I pack some clothes and my most valuable things into my school bag!"

"You know Raven you are a brave girl, it's a big risk you taken to tell us this, you do know that, you can't even go back to school!"

"I know, but I don't believe Giselle is doing the right thing luckily I'm not related to her, I want to do well with my magic like you!"

"Well it's always great to have another on our side, you can help us find a counter curse!" Miranda said.

"And the missing gemstone!" Rachel added.

"Oh, I forgot we're part the way there!" Raven reached into her pocket and pulled out a map. "Here, it's a little complicated though I was hoping it made more sense to you!" She handed Anne the map, Miranda and the others also studied it.

"Where did you get this?" Angie asked.

"Giselle has it, I stole it and made a copy at school. I've been trying to solve it for weeks now, my original plan was finding the gemstone myself and bringing it straight to you, but it's too hard for me!"

"Why didn't you tell me that before?" Roxy said.

"Because I knew you didn't trust me, and also I still had to live there with them, so long as I didn't tell anyone then it wasn't betrayal.

"You are a smart girl!" Anne said. The look on her face made it clear she was impressed with Raven.

"I think it best if we took them all out of school. Giselle will soon realise what's happened, and our children will be the first ones she'll go to for answers!" Rachel said.

"That's true, Roxy texted them all to come here immediately," Anne ordered. Roxy got straight to texting the others, and got frustrated when she received replies from them all asking why. Eventually they did as they were ordered and when they were all at the house, Anne and the other witch elders set to explaining the situation.

Seventeen

Nightfall began to descend on Sanford. Drake and the others began to wake from their sleep. As Drake climbed the stone steps from the dungeons to the main part of the house, he heard the witches engaging in a very heated discussion. He listened outside the door to the living room for a moment. He had missed the bit of conversation that had specified what they were discussing, so with that he entered the room. As he did, they all instantly stopped talking.

"I thought I made it quite clear ladies, that there's to be no secrets!" he said. None of them answered him. "So then do tell, what are you planning to hide from me!"

"Nothing my lord!" Giselle answered.

"Don't lie to me; I don't think I have to explain the consequences of that mistake now do I!"

"It's Raven my lord!" Giselle began to speak but was interrupted by Missy.

"No Mother don't," Missy begged. Drake shot a look of intense hatred at Missy.

"She's gone, she never returned from school and some of her things are missing."

"So the little brat has run away!" Drake said. "What are you planning on doing about it?"

"There's more my lord, I have reason to believe she has gone to the other witches!"

"Well you know the penalty for treason, so you better be sure that these accusations are correct!" Drake approached Giselle and stood over her. "I'm sure you wouldn't want that fate for your youngest daughter now would you, and you know what they say about treason, it runs in the family!" Drake moved away from Giselle and stood near the fireplace.

"She's not my daughter!" Giselle revealed.

"What!" Drake was enraged by this. "Then who is she?"

"She's an orphan; her family were killed in a fire when she was five. We came across while passing through some years ago!"

"And where was this?"

"Here in Sanford!" Drake took a moment to digest this information.

"I want her found as soon as possible and brought straight to me!"

"What will you do to her?" Missy asked.

"Oh I'm sure you can guess!" With that Drake left the room. Missy sat in the armchair in shock, she'd always been close to Raven, and she saw her as a daughter, even if Giselle didn't. Missy was torn by her own family and the young girl she adored, and more or less raised herself.

Eighteen

Missy was in her room pacing. She hadn't yet decided what she should do. It was clear when Missy was young that she wasn't like her mother and sister. She had more kindness in her, and care for others. When Missy was a teenager she had questioned whether Giselle was really her mother. And when they had come across Raven, she believed it even more.

Her childhood wasn't great either. Crystal always got better things, and their mother clearly favoured her more than Missy. Both of them tormented Missy, and most nights Missy would cry herself to sleep. She never told her mother how she felt, she guessed she wouldn't care and it would give them more reason to torment her. She sat on the edge of her bed and wondered why she had stayed with them for so long, why hadn't she left when she was old enough to take care of herself, which would have been when Missy was 12 maybe 13 years old. She put her head in her hands, and sobbed as she recalled her terrible childhood. After a few minutes she reached for a tissue on her bedside table, and wiped the tears from her eyes. She looked up and caught a glance of herself in the mirror. For a moment she saw the sad lonely girl she once was, and realised that she wasn't lonely any more, she had Raven, and that she was now an adult and didn't have to stay with her mother and sister if she didn't want, although leaving would have risks. But she thought when it came to options the hardest option was always the one worth sticking with, and that only cowards chose easy options, afraid of risks, and consequences. With that in mind she stood up and went to her wardrobe, she found a bag and packed some things, and also grabbed her coat. She looked at herself one last time before she headed towards the door, and smiled. She finally saw a reflection of herself that she could be proud of. As she approached the door she pressed her ear against it, when she was happy she couldn't hear anyone outside she slowly opened it.

Before she stepped into the corridor she looked left and then right. Apart from old pictures and an oak table with a vase on it, (it was old and obvious no flowers had been in it for a long time), it was empty. She crept to the right careful of her footing, making sure she didn't step on any creaking floorboards. She reached the stairs, and again paused and listened for any movement below. It was dark, the stairs led to the kitchen, she was sure none of the vampires would be down there, but she was unsure of Giselle or Crystal. With no light coming up from the kitchen she was confident no one was down there. Again she crept slowly down, her heart began to race, when she finally realised what she was doing. None of the witches in the castle could leave without permission and stating their reason. Going out at night was forbidden, if she was caught, even by her family she would severely punished. She shook the thought out of her mind, there was no going back now, she'd had enough, and it was time she escaped and set herself free, and do good with her magic not evil.

She entered the kitchen and quickly made her way towards the door; as she suspected it was unlocked. Why would vampires need to lock the doors, especially when there was spell around the building preventing enemies to enter? As she grabbed the door handle to finally escape, she heard some movement coming from the living room next door. She froze, and her heart was beating so fast it felt as though it would burst through her chest. She began to feel butterflies in her stomach. When she hadn't heard anything for a minute or so, she opened the door just enough for her to fit through, when she was outside she closed the door as slowly and quietly as possible. She turned and ran as fast as she could to the main gates that were open as the vampires had left earlier. She walked along the country lane not knowing where she would go when she got into town. She walked down the streets that led into the middle of town, she knew now after a half an hour of walking that she was looking for a werewolf, and hoping that she didn't run into any of the vampires at the same time. While walking down Rhombold Avenue she noticed two boys at the end of the street. They looked to be around the same age as Raven, they had noticed her too. As she got closer to them she called to them.

"Hey, I was wondering if you boys could help me!" They began to approach her, and she knew they must be werewolves. They didn't speak to her. "Hi, are you boys werewolves?"

"How'd you know about werewolves?" the taller of the two asked.

"I'm a witch!" As Missy answered she rolled up her sleeve revealing the mark on her wrist, the two boys nodded to each other. She looked closely at the shorter boy, he looked familiar somehow, but she couldn't quite place him in her mind. "I'm looking for a young witch, Raven, do you know her?" The two boys suddenly seemed alarmed, she could sense anger in their eyes and she knew what that meant.

"Are you from the castle?" Again it was the tall boy who spoke.

"Yes, but I swear I'm no threat or enemy to you, I just want to find her, to see if she's OK!"

"She's fine, go back to your castle!" The boys turned to leave.

"So you know where she is, she's helping you isn't she?" She knew that she had chosen the wrong words and the taller boy spun round, strode towards her and grabbed her arm.

"So what if she is, has that ruined your plans, does she know too much and you're afraid you're going to fail. The vampires won't like that will they!" He let go of her and turned back to join his friend.

"I want to help too, Raven is the closest thing I have to family right now...!" Both boys stopped, but didn't turn around. "I brought her up like she was my own, my mother didn't really care, please, I beg you!" The boys didn't seem as though they were listening to her, they seemed distracted somehow. Missy listened and she could hear footsteps behind her.

"Well, well, Missy, what are you doing out at night!" Missy turned around, she was face to face with Carlos. She heard a howl behind her, and a werewolf sprinted past her and pounced on Carlos. It started biting his arm; Carlos struggled but managed to get himself free, when he got up, he instantly took flight, and vanished. When the werewolf was sure the coast was clear he transformed back to his human self.

"Thank you!" Missy said, almost in a whisper.

"I'm Noah, this is Jack!" When she turned and looked Jack waved. They started walking and Missy didn't know whether to follow them.

"Are you coming or what, I'm sure there are plenty more of your vampire friends lurking about, and they can smell you!" Missy ran to catch up with them.

"Let's be clear on one thing, they are not my friends!"

"Glad to hear it!" Noah replied. As they walked it started to rain. She had no idea where they were taking her; she just knew by being with them she was safe.

"How come you didn't turn into a werewolf back there!" she asked Jack, making conversation.

"I'm not a werewolf!" he replied, knowing she would ask more questions.

"Did he rescue you too?"

"No!" Jack let it linger, as he imagined she was searching for her next question. "I'm a half breed if you will!"

"A half breed werewolf?" Missy asked.

"No, vampire!" Missy looked surprised and then she laughed as she found it hard to believe.

"He is, honest, he was conceived while his father was going through the turn!" Noah added.

"So what is a half breed exactly?" She was now intrigued.

"Well I have fangs, but no urge to drink blood, thank god, I have the sense of smell and great hearing, and I can walk around during the day!"

"I'd keep that last bit to yourselves, if the vampires knew that, they'd want a sample of your blood!" They reached an alley where two men were talking. Noah went to join them, Jack waited with Missy. Then it hit her, she realised why Jack looked so familiar, he was the spitting image of Isaac. While Noah had gone to talk to Caleb and Logan, Missy kept glancing over at Jack.

"What?" he asked.

"Nothing!" she replied. There was a moment of awkward silence. Then Missy spoke.

"Have you ever met your father it's just...!"

"Hey!" Caleb bellowed. He strode towards Missy, when he reached her, he led her away from Jack. "Don't tell him about his father!" Caleb turned to walk away.

"Isaac knows Jack is here, that's why they wanted his address, and he's not stupid, when he realises his son isn't home at night he will know, and go looking for him!"

"Yes, but we don't want Jack going looking for him, at the moment he has no desire to become a vampire, he's content with who he is!" She shrugged and nodded. Caleb ordered her to go with them, they didn't tell her where she was going and she didn't care just so long as it wasn't back to the castle. As they walked along the streets of Sanford the werewolves and Jack had made as circle around Missy. Caleb had told them that because Carlos had found Missy outside the castle at night, that alone would mean she couldn't go back, on top of that she had been seen with a werewolf. Caleb was confident that Carlos had also heard the conversation between Missy and the boys.

"It could still be a trap!" Logan whispered. Missy pretended that she didn't hear him.

"Logan, whether it is or isn't, we have no choice we are here to protect, if we leave her she will be the next victim," Caleb replied. He didn't whisper.

"This isn't a trap or anything like that, I already explained it to these two!" Missy bellowed. Logan held up his hands in a surrender type manner, and nodded his head.

"Missy don't yell, you'll attract unwanted attention!" Logan ordered. In the meantime Noah had been on his phone informing Roxy and the others what was going on.

Nineteen

The heavens opened and rain started to fall. The night was far from over. They'd had to take a detour; Noah had smelled a few vampires ahead of them. Logan was amazed as he hadn't picked up any scent, neither had Caleb, but he was glad that they finally had a hybrid on their side. It seemed as if they had walking all night; they had decided to head to the den. With all the vampires out in full force, even Drake, they needed to be sure that the risk they were taking was worth it. Greg was escorting Miranda to the den along with Joel and Tyler, Alex and Callum were still keeping watch over Lucy. As they reached the edge of the woods, they looked around to ensure that the coast was clear. When they were sure no one had followed them they entered the woods in silence.

The evening was growing tenser. They had to keep Missy safe, but at the same time ensure it wasn't a trap, so Caleb and Logan kept a close eye on her movements, to make sure she wasn't casting any curses or anything that could reveal their location. Missy had practised dark magic and that was something that was dangerous and also something that werewolves didn't fully understand, and because of that they feared it. With all of the vampire elders out of the castle stalking the streets, Caleb also didn't want to bump into any of them just in case they too saw the resemblance between Isaac and Jack. And running into Isaac himself was the situation Caleb was more anxious about. The rain got heavier, and the smell of the damp soil and bark from the trees began to fill the air in the woods. Noah could sense the tension. And he understood the situation; he made sure he was alert at all times. He knew Caleb was relying on him to smell and hear danger before Logan and himself. This was what he was wanting ever since he discovered he was a werewolf. Not that he was enjoying the moment too much though, deep down he was terrified of how the night was going end, and with that he could feel adrenalin following through his body, and taking over. He didn't think of it as a bad thing, he knew that it was making him more alert, more ready than ever to transform as he liked to call it. What he'd wanted was to be a part of it, and as it happened he was more important than any of the other werewolves. Caleb referred to him as his secret weapon, he tried to hide his own pride but he found it difficult. Along with that title came pressure not to let anyone down, after all he was still young and hadn't been a werewolf for very long. He still had a lot to learn and was still getting used to turning into a werewolf and back to a human again.

Back at the Moon house Raven was pacing the living room. Roxy, Lacy, Beth and Paige were trying to calm her but their efforts were useless. Anne, Rachel and Angie were sat in the kitchen focusing all their time in finding the gemstone. All three of them were secretly hoping Missy was genuine just like Raven. They knew their chances of finding the gemstone were greater if they had Missy on their side. They could hear Raven in the living room. Anne also understood how important Missy was to Raven and could guess that Raven was just as important to Missy. She could tell even though she'd never met Missy –

there was a mother daughter kind of bond between them, which was another reason she hoped it all wasn't a trap.

They were getting closer to the den. Noah knew his father was already there, he had picked up his scent. When they reached the entrance they took one final look to make sure they hadn't been followed. Since the night Noah and Roxy had followed their father here, Noah had learned that the werewolves only ever came here on a full moon, as part of a ritual; tonight was an exception. And even though werewolves weren't a threat to humans, when it came to their den they didn't like intruders, and just like wolves they got very territorial, it was the only time werewolves were a threat to humans. They walked along the tunnel they could hear the others talking.

"Hey guys!" Joel said. "How's your night going?"

"Oh it's going great Joel thanks for a asking!" Logan replied in a sarcastic manner. Miranda stared at Missy and looked her up and down. She convinced herself she was trying to figure her out, but the truth was she despised witches who kept the company of vampires. She didn't mind Raven, but then again she knew that Raven didn't really want to be there, and that good was Raven's true nature. Missy caught Miranda looking at her out of the corner of her eye.

"I know what you're thinking!" she said.

"Do you, not a surprise I must say!" Miranda replied.

"You're wrong!"

"We'll see, won't we?" Miranda walked towards Missy, she grabbed her hands just as she had done with Raven. The mist showed it was grey which meant it was unsure.

"Not looking too good for you at the moment is it!" Miranda hissed. Missy remained silent. Finally the grey mist started to change colour, it didn't go completely green like it had with Raven. It was mostly green but with slight streaks of red. Miranda let go of Missy's hands.

"What does that mean?" Caleb asked.

"It means there's a good nature and also a bad nature… but she chooses to act on the good, it's a lot stronger, that's why the mist was mainly green!"

"Well there's good and bad in all of us!" Logan added. Miranda nodded. She looked across to Missy.

"I suppose I owe you an apology!"

"No, I can understand your initial judgement. I have something I would like to share with you and the other witches, and it's about the gemstone!"

"I'll drive them back, you all need to get back to night watch," Greg said. Caleb agreed and they all followed him out of the den. Noah and Jack were ordered to take over from Alex and Callum while Tyler and Joel kept a watch on the rest of town. All four boys walked back into Sanford together. Logan and Caleb stayed in the woods for a moment. Tyler and Joel were filling Noah and Jack on their events of the evening. They too had bumped into Carlos and also Sebastian, Tyler and Joel had managed to fight them off, but Sebastian had injured Tyler on his leg, and with the pain he was limping.

"I wonder where Isaac is tonight?" Tyler asked.

"No idea, Drake is supposed to be lurking around somewhere too!" Noah replied.

"Yeah Logan told us, he said not to fight him if he showed his face!" Joel added.

"Why?" Jack asked out of curiosity.

"Well Drake is the leader, and he's also a pure breed vampire, he was born a vampire!" Joel replied.

"How, I mean how was he born a vampire!" Jack asked again still curious.

"Do you think it's strange how we never have encounters with female vampires?" Tyler said. "That's because they don't really leave the castle, they look after newly turned vampires, harvest people's blood, and also give birth to pure vampires!"

"Really?" Jack sounded surprised. "I just thought it was because there weren't any… I thought vampires were dead!"

"They are, well turned ones are anyway, no one really understands the pure breeds, to do that we'd have to kill one, and unfortunately that's never happed!" Tyler explained.

"That's not true… my dad killed Drake's father Charles!" Noah stated.

"But we didn't get hold of his body though, did we?" Tyler said. Noah shook his head. During conversation neither of them had noticed that they were being followed.

"Hello boys!" It was Josh, all four of them turned around. Josh stared at Jack. "So that's him then, you're on the wrong side mate you belong with us!" Joel stepped forward.

"No he doesn't. Will that be all Josh, because I reckon the four of us could rip you to pieces!" Josh looked from one to the other, realising he was outnumbered; he turned to leave.

"Oh just one more thing, your father is very disappointed Jack!" With that he instantly took flight.

"What!" Jack said in shock.

"Ignore him, the tosser!" Joel said. They continued their walk back into town. By the time Noah and Jack had reached Alex and Callum it was starting to get light. So they headed back home instead. Jack couldn't stop thinking about what Josh had said, the words kept replaying over and over in his mind. Ever since he found out he had vampire in him he'd always wondered if his father was up in the castle, but on the other hand he didn't know if Josh was winding him up, setting a trap so that he would be made to tell what he knew about Noah and the others.

Twenty

It had just turned eight o'clock in the morning when Noah finally got to bed. The events of the night before had everyone talking, and Missy had some important and Noah quite disturbing information. She had told them that the gemstone was hidden somewhere in the castle and would only reveal itself to heiress of the witch who made it. Anne had quickly come to the conclusion that Lucy was the heiress. Roxy had indeed been shocked by this and could not believe it, as Lucy hadn't expressed any knowledge of witches. Missy told her that Lucy's grandmother had died while her mother was still young and so therefore the power of their family had been lost. Of course Noah was also shocked by this and immediately requested permission to tell her with the help of Jack. Anne as always needed a little persuasion, but it didn't take as much as usual. She also agreed that when this was all over she would teach Lucy just like she taught Roxy.

Noah woke suddenly. He looked at the clock and shot out of bed when realised it was approaching lunchtime. He grabbed the clothes off the floor and threw them on, rushed into the bathroom and quickly washed his face and brushed his teeth. He didn't have anything to eat, he went straight out of the door. He headed straight for Lucy's house, he wasn't sure what he was going to say to her, but after what his mother had told him the night before he'd been getting immense feelings of anxiety because he was convinced something had happened while he'd been asleep. He quickened his pace. As soon as he reached the door he knocked heavily. Lucy's mother answered.

"Oh hello Noah... Would you like me to get Lucy!" she said a smooth, pleasant voice, but he could tell she had struggled to maintain it, as he could clearly see the tear tracks on her cheeks. Another argument he guessed, which was good news for him, Lucy was always desperate to get out of the house after her parents had argued, she hated the tension.

"Yes please!" Noah replied. When Lucy came to the door, just as he had suspected she didn't need much convincing. Together they went to Jack's. When they arrived, Noah knocked on the door, Lucy stood against the wall. To Noah and Lucy's surprise Jack's mother informed them that he went out early after Lucy had called round for him.

"Are you sure?" Noah asked looking confused.

"Yes dear, I'm sure I know what Lucy looks like of course!" Lucy was out of sight of Mary, and when she had told them Jack had left with her two hours ago she felt it best not to tell Mary that she had been at home all morning, and edged further away from the door.

Noah also didn't want to alarm Mary and replied, "OK thanks, I'm sure they're at the park or something!" After Mary had shut the door Lucy looked at Noah, she was worried, confused and wondered what was going on.

"I've been at home all morning, or am I going mad?" She spoke her thoughts out loud.

"No, you're not going mad!" Noah replied. "I think I know what's happened!" He was walking fast in the direction of his house; Lucy was struggling to keep up with him.

"Well... what's going on?"

"You won't believe me if I told you, so I'm going to get my family to help!" All the way back to Noah's, Lucy desperately trying to get answers, Noah kept telling her he will tell her when they got to his house. Finally they reached Noah's house and both of them strode in. Noah's family were in the sitting room, along with Raven and Missy, of course, as they were guests in the house. As soon as Noah entered the sitting room he told them what he had discovered.

"Jack is missing, I think the vampires have him!"

"What vampires have taken Jack, I think it's you that's gone mad!" Lucy said.

"How do know?" Greg asked. Noah told the conversation that he'd had with Mary. Lucy confirmed Noah's story was true and that she'd been at home all morning.

"Jack left his house with either my mother or Crystal, in Lucy's form!"

"Hey, come again?" Lucy said. "A women made herself look like me... How is that even possible?" Anne approached Lucy and told her to sit down; she explained everything. Lucy was in a bit of a daze while Anne told her that one of her friends was a werewolf and the other a half-breed vampire. She had learned all about the vampires, and witches. But the real shock came when Anne told her that she was a witch. Missy took over and told her all about her grandmother and the gemstone. She took it all in and the others were surprised with her response when she spoke for the first time in ten minutes. In that time the world had changed, her friends had changed, and also her thoughts about her dead grandmother.

"Alright so what do we do then?" Lucy asked. No one answered straight away, even though she seemed to have accepted everything she had been told, the others weren't sure if she thought it was a dream, or they were just winding her up.

"We need to protect you dear!" Anne finally spoke.

"And rescue Jack of course!" Noah added.

"That's an almost impossible task!" Greg said.

"But not entirely impossible!" Noah said. "He's my friend I have to at least try!" Greg final word was no, he will inform Caleb and see what he decides, until then Noah was deemed house bound. Just as Missy and Raven had Lucy became a guest at the Moon house. She didn't go home straight away to get her things, instead Roxy had asked to speak with her.

"I'm sorry about how I have treated you!" Roxy said. Lucy said nothing at first, she just stood in front of Roxy with her arms folded and listened to Roxy apologise more. This had begun to make Lucy slightly agitated.

"You're only sorry because now you know I'm just like you, if it weren't for that you wouldn't be sorry!" Roxy knew that was true but not entirely so she tried to explain the reason why she seemed to dislike her so much.

"Some witches have the ability to read minds and things like that, I think I sensed somehow that you are a witch but the bad kind, it was only when Missy told us about you that I realised that was the reason!"

"How do you know I'm bad?" Roxy shrugged at Lucy's question. "I have very different feelings about my grandmother, before today I'd wished that I could have known her, and felt sad and angry that she died at a young age... Now I'm glad I didn't know her, and she got what she deserved!" Lucy's tone had relaxed a bit, and become slightly friendlier.

"I could tell that when my mum told you, the look on your face was a look of disappointment but most of all disapproval!" Lucy looked at the floor, Roxy could see the tears begin to fill her eyes. She placed her hand on her shoulder. "I have no idea what it that must feel like... I imagine terrible, but if you want to talk don't hesitate, us good witches stick together and look after each other!"

"Thanks, I'm sorry too, but with everything going on and with Noah, it just drove me a little crazy!" Roxy gave Lucy a hug and told her not to worry, that being a witch was like having a second family. She also made hints that Noah still liked her. Lucy smiled at the thought and decided she should go home and get some things before nightfall, after what she just heard she really didn't want be wandering the streets at night. She told Anne where she was going, Anne made the suggestion that Roxy should give her lift, but Lucy declined she wanted to go alone and let it all sink in.

When Lucy got home both her parents were watching TV, they liked to watch soaps and game shows. Lucy told her mother that she was staying at Noah's for a few nights because his parents were away; her mother just nodded her head. She climbed the stairs and turned left along the landing to her room, she opened the door, once inside she closed it behind her. She hadn't noticed the figure standing in the corner left of the door because she had turned right. On her dresser next to her wardrobe was a glass of water, she took a sip but didn't look up in the mirror. After a few minutes she began to feel dizzy and light headed, slowly her vision started to go blurry. She turned around and dropped the clothes in her hands, she was looking at herself, as she started fall to floor, the figure changed before her eyes. Before her eyes completely shut, she saw a short, plump woman with black hair that was grey in some places, and straw like. It was Giselle.

Twenty-One

Noah was pacing his room, while Roxy sat on his bed running her hair through her fingers. It was clear to them both that Lucy had now fallen prisoner to the vampires. She had been gone far too long and it was getting dark. They were now discussing ways to get into the castle and rescue Lucy and Jack. There was a knock on the door.

"Hey, I want in on this!" Raven said, as she stepped into the room, she sat next to Roxy. "After all, I lived in the castle for some time, and you can bet I explored it!" Noah and Roxy both agreed that she could help. She asked Noah for piece of paper and a pen, when he handed them to her she began to draw a map of the castle. She mainly focused on the dungeon and the first floor. After she had finished she pointed to a trap door, situated on the exterior of the castle.

"This is the best way in!" she said. "It leads directly into the corridor of the dungeon!" She pointed on the map she also located the rooms in which the vampires slept during the day. "Obviously we should enter during the day, but you still have to beware that it's pitch black down there, so the vampires can come out of their coffins and walk around, as you know they have great hearing, but so does Noah!"

"What about the defensive charm?" Roxy asked.

"Missy gave me a counter curse, very simple, especially since I've been in the castle before, it shouldn't recognise me as a threat!"

"Brilliant!" Noah said. "I think we need Joel and Tyler as well!"

"Good idea, but only those two, the counter curse won't work for any more than five, it will view it as an ambush!" Raven explained.

As the sun was rising over Sanford, Noah, Roxy and Raven were already on their way to meet Joel and Tyler. Roxy drove to the other end of town, neither of them spoke, Noah had become anxious and was fidgeting in his seat. Eventually Noah caught sight of Joel's pick up, and he wasn't sure if he got more anxious or excited. Roxy parked her car next to Joel's and they all got out.

"You ready!" Noah said to Joel.

"Yep we are!" Joel replied. "Aren't we!" He turned to Tyler. Tyler nodded. They walked down the country lane towards the gate that leads into the courtyard of the castle. Raven and Roxy chatted the whole way, the boys remained quiet. When they reached the gate they hesitated, as they all realised once they were on the other side of it that there was no turning back. Joel slowly edged the gate open, as he did it creaked. He opened it just enough so they could get through. They crept around the side of the castle to the back, they made sure not to be seen and ducked under the windows as they went past. When they reached the wooden hatch Raven stood facing the castle. She mumbled something to herself, and then out loud she said, "Good will wins!" Then she bent down and opened the hatch. The others followed but found that they couldn't enter the castle. "You all have to say what I said before I entered!" Roxy was the first, she repeated the phrase and entered the castle. Noah, Joel and Tyler soon followed.

"Why did we have to say that to get inside?" Noah asked.

"I wasn't sure what would happen if I removed the charm completely because Giselle does plan for those things, so I just changed the pass phrase!"

"Fair enough, where do we go now?" Joel asked looking down a rather narrow, damp and dark corridor. There were ten doors five on each side and one at the end opposite them. They each had a torch as it was pitch black. Raven lowered her voice almost to a whisper.

"Try to keep quiet along here, these rooms are where the vampires sleep, not the elders though!" She started walking towards the door at the end, she turned to look at the others, they didn't seem alarmed by her information. "I told you earlier because it's dark it doesn't matter whether it's day or night, they can walk around down here!" The others exchanged glances and followed her. When Raven reached the door at the end she pressed her ear up against it. She waited a moment and then opened it. It was lighter in this part of the dungeon, as there were lamps on the walls.

"No, it can't be!" Raven said. She moved to the left and walked past all the rooms, she stopped to think.

"What, what's wrong!" Roxy asked.

"This is where they keep their prisoners locked up, and they're all empty, if Jack and Lucy aren't here then Giselle must have started the ritual!"

"Are we too late?" Noah asked.

"There's a good chance that we're not, just depends on when Giselle started it. It's a long and complicated task, especially when there's as many vampires as there are here. Noah headed towards the door at the end of the corridor.

"Noah what are you doing?" Raven asked.

"I can hear voices!" He pushed his ear against the door. "They're in there!" he said. The others quickly joined his side. Noah nodded and they entered the room. Crystal, Giselle, Drake and Sebastian all turned to look when they burst in. Lucy was tied down to a cross that had been placed on a table. Giselle stood over her with the gemstone in her hand. The gemstone was smaller than Noah had imagined. It was the size of a pebble, but it was glowing, and Raven knew that wasn't a good thing, not for Lucy. She turned to Noah and whispered to him.

"It's nearly complete; all they need now is Lucy's blood!" Noah began to feel anger and rage take over his body. He glanced at Joel and Tyler and they instantly knew what they had to do, although it was a dangerous risky move as they could only take werewolf form at night. Then unexpectedly Noah turned, Tyler and Joel were surprised, and so was Drake.

"Impossible!" Drake bellowed. "It's him he's the one!" With that Sebastian leapt into action, and within a matter of seconds Noah and Sebastian were locked in a death grip. Noah knew he couldn't let him go, he had to enforce fear in vampires and this was how to do it, kill a leader. Something no young werewolf had ever done. It took years of experience, but he knew he could. In the meantime, Roxy and Raven attacked Giselle. They jumped on her and Roxy grabbed the gemstone and placed it in her pocket. Raven stood up and cursed Giselle, and it seemed as though Giselle had turned to stone, she couldn't move. Crystal came forward.

"STOP!" Raven yelled. "Do you want to end up like that?" Crystal shook her head. Roxy bound her legs and arms with the rope that was used on Lucy.

"You have a dark gift Raven!" Roxy said. "I like it!" Joel ordered the girls to get out and run. They did what they were told and ran for the exit. Noah and Sebastian were still fighting. Noah grabbed Sebastian by the neck and lifted him off the ground. He lifted up his left paw, and slammed it into Sebastian's chest impaling him. Noah knew he'd stuck in the right place, he could hear Sebastian heart start to slow down, until there was nothing. Noah released his grip and Sebastian's body fell to the floor, and it lay there lifeless. Noah looked down at him, and then glanced up at Drake. He could tell by his eyes he was terrified, he knew what Drake's weakness was, what he feared the most and it was him. He approached Drake and as he did he slashed him with his claw, Drake staggered backwards.

"No please, I'm sorry!" Drake said. To Tyler and Joel's surprise. Noah turned back to human form. He stepped closer to Drake.

"I know what you're afraid of!" Noah said. "Since the night I became a werewolf I have felt your presence, I've had visions, you're afraid of me!"

"You're different from the others, stronger!"

"And you have your father to thank for that!" Noah replied. "Now where is Jack?"

"It's too late for him, you were wrong about what he is!" Drake replied.

"Don't lie to me, it only makes me angry!"

"He's not!" Jack said. Noah turned around and Jack was stood in the doorway. "The process was slower that's all, now I'm a vampire!"

"No mate you can't!" Tyler said.

"I'm sorry I wish I wasn't, this is where I belong now!" Jack said. "You have to go!" Noah found it hard to believe, but knew he had to go. Tyler and Joel followed. Just before they left the room Noah turned around to face Drake.

"I want you to leave my town at sunset, if you don't I will be back!" And then he left.

Noah went home he knew he would be in trouble but he didn't care. When he finally walked through the door with Tyler and Joel close behind him, he sat down and told everyone what happened, and to his surprise his parents were proud of him. As night fell on Christmas Eve, he imagined the vampires fleeing in fear, although a big part of him did believe that they would stay. As everyone sat round the Christmas tree, Noah went to the kitchen. He glanced out of window as he sat at the table. As he gazed into the dark he thought he saw a silhouette of someone stood in his garden and went outside to investigate. But no one was there, he came to the conclusion that he had imagined it, and turned to go inside.

"See you mate!" Noah turned around to find Jack stood in front of him. "We're going like you asked, after what you did to Sebastian, Drake is too afraid to stay!"

"You don't have to go!" Noah said.

"I have to; I belong with them, with my dad!"

"Well then take care, of yourself!"

"And you take care of Sanford and of course Lucy!" With that Jack walked away, and then disappeared. Noah had mixed emotions, he felt pleased he'd driven the vampires away, but sad and slightly devastated that his best friend was leaving with them.

THE END